BREAK MY BONES
RACHAEL TAMAYO

TANGLED TREE
PUBLISHING
tangledtreepublishing.com

BREAK MY BONES © 2019 by RACHAEL TAMAYO

For information, contact the publisher, Tangled Tree Publishing.

WWW.TANGLEDTREEPUBLISHING.COM

EDITING: HOT TREE EDITING

COVER DESIGNER: BOOKSMITH DESIGN

FORMATTING: RMGRAPHX

E-book ISBN: 978-1-925-853-51-3

Paperback ISBN: 978-1-925853-52-0

BREAK MY BONES

RACHAEL TAMAYO

A DEADLY SINS NOVEL ⬟

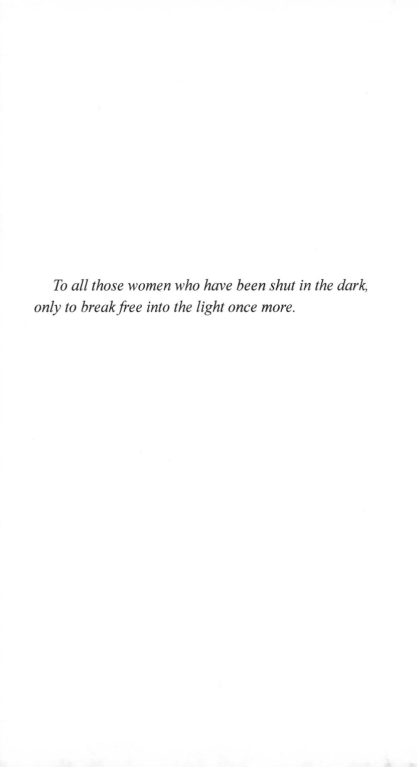

*To all those women who have been shut in the dark,
only to break free into the light once more.*

The Sin of Wrath

"Holding anger is a poison. It eats you from inside. We think that hating is a weapon that attacks the person who harmed us. But hatred is a curved blade. And the harm we do, we do to ourselves."

—MITCH ALBOM, *The Five People You Meet in Heaven*

Chapter One

CAIN

Seventy-Two Hours Ago

CAIN, BABY, WAKE UP.

Open your eyes, love.

Cain....

The sweet voice caresses my ear, sliding around my body like smooth satin. The light, clean scent of her perfume pulls my lips up in a smile. Reaching for her, I find nothing but air. I roll, and the squeak of the cot and the pain in my back from the shitty mattress remind me of where I am.

The fuzzy warmth from the dream fades, replaced with the chill in the room. The blanket is too small for my long frame, so I wear socks to bed. The perfume is now the musty, dank smell of mold and piss.

I don't want to open my eyes, but my full bladder forces me to. The undercarriage of the bunk above me hovers before my eyes as I struggle to focus and clear the dream from the reality that is my life. I sit up, planting my feet on the floor, ducking to avoid hitting my head. The concrete floor is cold through my socks as I walk toward the stainless-steel toilet in the corner of my cell. My surroundings are nothing but a reminder of the fact that she's out there without me while I've been stuck in here.

If I'm honest with myself—and I rarely am—I belong here. In jail, away from her. She probably felt my fist more often than she did my cock in the years we were married.

No, not were. We still are married. She's still mine, and always will be. No one can change that. Nothing but death.

"So, today's the big day." His rough voice invades my thoughts of Brooklyn, and I hate him for it. I wish he'd leave me to my fantasies.

I turn to him, pulling my pants up. My cellmate tosses a ball, bouncing it off the ceiling without looking at me. He plays this game constantly. It used to drive me insane, but I learned to live with it, even almost enjoy it. Now I get to sleep to the sound of the rhythmic thumping at night.

"Yeah, it is." I turn my back on the five-star bathroom facilities, hating his smiling face for no real reason.

"Come on, aren't you excited? The free world? Sunshine, sex, Jim Beam. I know you've missed it."

I pass by my box of crap, packed and ready to go. I'm getting out today. My three years are up; I'm a free man once again. Her picture lies on top of the box, beautiful as she holds our newborn daughter for the first time. Her chocolate-brown eyes reflect a smile that sparkles with motherhood. Maybe today will be the day I get to see her again, see both of them again.

"It has been a while." I glance up at my cellmate. Jim Beam is what landed me in here. Pissed, drunk as fuck, and behind the wheel. My third arrest for DWI, so they let me know they meant business this time. Donovan was with me that night, but he got away. We grew up together, but I don't blame him for running. I would've done the same, had he been pegged instead of me. He's been at my side since I was twelve years old. His friendship got me through when my dad took off and my mom checked out, having better things to do than be a mother to me. I use the term friendship loosely. What you would call childhood friendship was more like a twisted dependence on my part. Lacking affection, attention, a real male role model, I clung to him as a boy. Now it's turned into this love-hate thing. Friendship? Brotherhood? I just don't know what to call it. Maybe brotherhood is a good word, because you can hate a brother and love him at the same time.

Jim Beam. The name brings back a phantom of flavor, the ache for the taste. The years in jail have given me time to dry out, but the craving is still there. The longing for the burn, for the numbness. It's the only thing that helps the headaches I get, or kills the itch of guilt when I think about what I've done.

3

What *she* made me do. What *he* made me do.

What might've happened? Would I have ended up here if not for Donovan and his constant bullshit? What course might my life have taken? Would I have ever hurt her had it not been for him? There were his taunts, of course, but also the simple fact that he's the only one who's ever stuck with me, which gives me the inclination to listen to him, him being just a little older and wiser. When my dad took off, my mom turned into a money-grubbing whore, leaving me to my own devices. Donovan picked me up, brushed me off, and made me a man.

Though he made me a man I hate, and I loathe him for it. But I also don't know how to cut him out of my life, so here I am, on my last day in jail, because of something he got me involved in.

My cellmate laughs at me. "Don't look at me like that. It's not my fault you ended up here." He misunderstands the look on my face. We've talked about a lot since I arrived, but I never mentioned Donovan to him. He doesn't know about all that.

I fall onto my bunk with a groan. "Fuck you."

He laughs.

I remain silent. Convicted of DWI, pegged with assault. In the end, the assault charges didn't stick, eventually dropped. The assault on the bartender that night, not her, my wife. A bartender who should've minded his own business but instead decided to call the cops on Donovan and me after the bar fight. Not the first time we started shit up and took off, but that time we got caught. Or I did anyway.

I can't begin to tell you how many times we *didn't* get caught over the years.

"Hey, you're done, right? Today you can get out, get fucked, and go grovel your way back into your little wifey's bed."

Finding her, looking into her eyes and holding her in my arms, I'd most definitely grovel. I'd beg. I didn't mean to hurt her, but I can't control it when I get angry. She knows that's how I am, but she pushed my buttons anyway. Maybe now, after this cooling off period, we've both learned a thing or two and can start over. Restart our lives together.

When I met Donovan as a kid, he was the first to tell me the truth about things. Made me understand that no one would be there for me except me, and possibly him. He taught me to lean on him, and yet somehow always be skeptical of everyone. Trust no one, depend on no one, except myself. His companionship over the years, his *life lessons*, taught me just that. But the same way a hard-ass, jaded father might teach such a lesson to a son, the student still ends up leaning on the teacher, the master. Donovan is one sick fuck of a sensei, or a father figure, but he did what my own mother never could. I had to take respect if I wanted it. It became clear that he was right as I watched my mom spiral down further and further with every strange man she let into her bed. Each time she let one of them hit me and turned away without a word. My twelve-year-old self looked up to him at sixteen, because he knew everything. He was my idol. It was just me and Donovan against the world. He's the only one who's stayed with me after my mom, my dad, even Brook turned their backs on me. I still have a hate for him that I just can't shake, but I live with it. My cross to bear, as they say. The price I pay for having one loyal friend who I can trust.

I hate that he was right. I so hoped he would be wrong about her. My bride. My love. She looked me dead in the eyes and lied to me. I knew once she did that it was too late. At least that's what I thought then. But she let me down just like the rest of them. Every last one.

***

It was sheer luck that I discovered it. The hidden money. Going to make a withdrawal from my account, forgetting my account number, my debit card. When the teller looked up my name and social security number, she asked me, "Which account would you like to withdraw from, sir?" Confused, I took the paper she slid across the desk. Sure enough, two accounts. A new one opened using the information from our first account. A separate savings account with almost four hundred dollars in it.

Lifting my eyes, I look up at the young, pretty teller

and smile. "Both, honey. Thank you."

I walk out of the bank, almost slamming right into Donovan who's outside smoking. Seeing the look on my face, he tucks a lock of hair behind his ear and asks me what's up. I tell him on the way to the car, growing angrier all the way home. I grip the steering wheel until my knuckles go white. I listen to his reasoning, gritting my teeth. "She's going to leave you. She thinks you're a fool. What are you going to do about this?"

Leave me. *The words stop my breathing. She can't leave me. Find someone new, look at me and laugh, take my child from me. My daughter. I won't let it happen.*

My hands start to shake, trembling as I light a cigarette, tossing the lighter onto the dash. "Let's get a drink and think this over," Donovan suggests, directing me into the parking lot of a bar. I turn, unable to do anything but think of her laughing at me, taking my child and walking off, fucking another man.

By the time I leave the bar, I'm half drunk, murderous, and sad that it's come to this. Donovan leaves me to my task, waving me off. I left him sitting alone, going to my car and pulling the 9mm out from under my seat. My chest hurts. The weapon is heavy in my hand as I wonder if this is right. Maybe I should sleep on it. I don't want to live without her.

Live without her. Fuck that.

I slide out the clip. It's loaded. Enough for her and me. I won't have to live without her. Maybe on the other side, we can finally be happy.

I start the car and head home, glancing at the gun in the seat beside me all the way home. But what about Carissa? My mom will take her, I guess. I'll make sure she's safe before the final pull of the trigger.

I toss the spent cigarette butt out the window, lighting another with shaking hands as I pull onto my street.

* * *

No one could ever have her but me, but she didn't respect me. I'll get respect from her one way or another, or I'll kill her and me both. I meant it then, and I think I still mean it now.

I can't live without her, and I won't let her live without me.

The jingle of keys, the clang of metal on metal, and then the door opens. The guard stands to the side, shoving his keys in his pocket. "Free at last, free at last. Lawd almighty, you're free at last." He stops to guffaw at his own joke, hitching his belt up over his fat ass. "Time to go do your paperwork. Get your ass out of my jail." He smiles like a proud father shoving a baby bird out of the nest, not releasing a monster back into society.

"Bye, sweetie." My cellmate blows me a kiss, then goes back to tossing the ball. I walk out, the door slamming heavily behind me. The ball slapping on the ceiling fades as I follow the guard.

After processing, I walk out in the same clothes I wore that night, jeans and a T-shirt, wallet in a plastic bag. They gave me enough money for a cab, nothing more. Squinting into the sunlight, I glance around and see him sitting on the bench.

"'Bout time," he says, taking a drag off a cigarette and then grinding it out under his boot. He raises his sunglasses, revealing his dark eyes, his black, shaggy hair now longer, almost to his shoulders.

"I can't believe you showed up."

He shrugs. "I had nothing better to do. Come on, let's go get her." He stands, then turns to me. "You do want to, don't you? Go get her?"

"Damn right. She's still my wife. She'll always be—"

He walks off, but only after rolling his eyes at me. "I know, I know. Let's go."

She better be ready 'cause I'm coming, with Donovan right behind me.

***

BROOKLYN

PRESENT DAY

The click of the gun makes me jump.

I bolt up, wide-eyed and panting, glancing around as I will my heart to stop pounding. I'm home in bed, my five-year-old daughter, Carissa, asleep beside me, having snuck into my room yet again.

I swallow, brushing sweaty locks of hair off my neck and reaching for the glass of water on the nightstand.

Will these dreams ever stop? I rub under my chin where I felt the cold steel before waking, the feeling haunting me. A phantom 9mm making sweat roll down my spine.

Too bad it wasn't just a dream.

I toss back the comforter, worn thin before I ever got it at the Salvation Army. Carissa snuggles deeper under the black flowery monstrosity, thrusting out her long legs as I get out of bed. After double-checking she's still asleep, I kneel on the floor and reach under the bed, as is my ritual when these dreams come.

Reaching into the black void, I pull out the biometric safe with both hands, careful not to make any noise. I scan my fingerprint and the door opens, revealing cash totaling nearly five thousand dollars next to my gun. I pull the weapon out and then push the safe back under the bed, just in case she wakes up.

I bought the gun as soon as I bought the car, with the money I got when we were rescued from all those months living on the streets after we ran. I swore I'd never be without a way to defend us ever again.

Those were the worst months of my life. I went from one kind of hell straight into another, but I had to get away. That night will be with me for the rest of my life. The night my daughter saved me from eating the bullet my husband was determined to shove down my throat.

My bare feet sink into the worn beige carpeting as I stand up. I have to search the apartment. I know he's in jail, but I still have to search the place.

I can't sleep until I make sure we're alone.

I finger the safety as I check the locks, then the closets, cabinets, and every other place a person might be able to squeeze their body into—not to mention a few that even the smallest person couldn't fit, let alone him. The last time I saw him, he needed to lose fifty pounds, but I can't rest until I've looked everywhere; who knows what he looks like since he's been in prison. Once I'm satisfied we're alone, I replace the weapon in the safe, putting it back in its hiding place before grabbing my phone.

It's almost 5:00 a.m. I don't have to be at work for hours yet, but she'll be waking for school before I can get back to sleep. I know there's no point in lying back down, because I won't sleep. I hardly ever do after one of those dreams.

Memories of struggling to find comfort on the cold pavement while holding a sleepy three-year-old will haunt me until I die. I didn't sleep then. How could I? I was terrified I'd wake up and she'd be gone, snatched away or worse. I'd go days without sleeping, only finally allowing it when my tips would afford us a shitty motel room for the night. It's the reason so many women don't run. They have no place to go. Everyone tosses out those pretty words offering help, but the system just isn't set up to keep all those promises, and more often than not, they end up stranded in a women's shelter, or worse. Just like I did.

I need help, some kind of therapy. I know I do. I make coffee and turn on the TV, knowing I'll probably never reach out for the support I need to really overcome it all. Stubborn to a fault.

That stubbornness used to be what set him off. My loving husband. I'd pop off and get a mouth full of blood for it.

Carissa will never know what happened if I have any say in the matter. She won't ever know she saved my life when she was only a toddler. That I ran for my life from her father with nothing, then fled the homeless shelter because they were calling the authorities to take her away from me. She's going to be smart. Smarter than me.

The alarm goes off to get Carissa ready for school, and I set my third cup of coffee on the table. I turn the TV from the news to SpongeBob and commence with pissing off my little girl.

I pull the covers back, knowing a gentle hand will never wake up this child. She moans, reaching for blankets that are now well out of reach. "Get up, girlie.

Time for school." She groans in protest, grabbing the pillow and hiding under it. I laugh, turning on the light and removing the offending pillow. "Baby, get up. Come on." I pat her leg and walk off.

A few moments later, I hear her footsteps padding down the hall, her exaggerated collapse on the couch with one eye cracked, watching cartoons. A bowl of cereal later, she's awake and pulling on her clothes in front of the TV as I check her backpack and pack her lunch.

After taking her to school, I return to our two-bedroom apartment and change my clothes to begin my daily ritual. I run for miles, only returning to change my sweat-soaked shirt for a fresh one before heading for a women's kickboxing class. After that, I go to the gym at my apartment complex for weight lifting. Three hours a day, every day, no matter what. When I swore that I'd never be without the ability to defend myself, I meant it. If he ever finds us, I'll be ready.

I know he won't be in prison forever. I never called the police after what he did, just ran once he was behind bars. The women's shelters demanded that I call them in order to stay, but I knew the police would call Child Protective Services on me and I'd lose Carissa. I couldn't let my baby end up in the hands of CPS. Probably a selfish decision on my part, but I couldn't risk her getting placed with a sick foster parent where she'd be hurt, molested, neglected, or even worse. I had to keep her with me to keep her safe. I couldn't have it any other way. Even now I always know who she's with. No running around outside up and down the streets, no way. I don't see her as much as I want, working such crazy hours, but she's always safe. Never alone, never out of sight of someone I trust with the life of my little girl. Someone who knows the truth.

This is what I do to protect us. I live with this PTSD or OCD or whatever the hell it is, praying Carissa doesn't pick up on my bad habits, begging God that he'll make her smarter than I was so she never ends up in a situation like mine.

After a shower and a protein shake, I head to work. The people who rescued me, Ashley and Shane, also gave me a job at their business. I started as a waitress, and over the last three years, I've worked my way up to manager of The Blue Room, their club in downtown Dallas. Ashley is like a sister to me now, and since she stays home to watch her own son, she also watches Carissa for me while I work at night. Without them, I don't know where I'd be. Ashley knows where I came from, what I ran from, and I know she would protect Carissa. I'd never leave her with anyone else, ever.

It's almost eleven on a Friday night, so it's busy as hell in here. The bartender asked me for a case of Miller Light, and I'm returning from the fridge with it when I see him. He's only here a couple of times a month, and he seems to know my boss. That's actually where the man is now, huddled with Shane about ten feet from the front door.

I swallow, forcing my feet to move again as I wonder what it is about this tall blond man that always catches my attention. He stands with his thick arms crossed over a broad chest, wearing a long-sleeved T-shirt and well-worn jeans. Light eyes look away from Shane, scanning the room until they land on me.

He looks me over, then meets my eyes. Even from this distance, I get a chill. I bite my lip, and he smiles at me and nods in recognition. I don't do anything, just keep walking toward the bar and glancing over at him to see if he's still watching me. He is. I turn my head to hide my smile as I go back to the bar with the beer.

He never approaches me, and I can't help but wonder why. Maybe he's with someone, or even married. Either way, I suppose it doesn't matter. It's not like I'd ever do anything. I don't need to have a man in my life to worry about. One was enough. Hell, he was enough for a lifetime.

After I hand off the beer, I turn again, finding Shane and the handsome stranger missing from their place by the door. I scan the room, then chastise myself before heading back to work.

Chapter Two

CAIN

FORTY-EIGHT HOURS AGO

THE ROOM TIPS AND SPINS ONCE AGAIN. My mouth tastes like slow-aged Tennessee whiskey and cigarettes.

Speaking of, I pull out the pack in my pocket, shake one loose, and light it just as I stumble in the front door of our small two-bedroom rental. The house is dark.

"She didn't even leave the light on for you." Donovan laughs much too loudly as he stumbles and reaches for the light, blinding me with the sudden brightness thrown from the bulb overhead.

My stomach growls. The red bud glows as I inhale until I start coughing out the putrid drag of smoke, pushing it out of my lungs. "There better be food."

He follows me to the kitchen, turning on all the lights as he goes. I check the oven—it's empty. I'm still holding the door open when Donovan laughs.

"She didn't keep it warm. Useless bitch." He opens the door to the fridge and pulls out my plate, tearing off the foil and stuffing a whole corn bread muffin into his face.

I told her to leave the light on. And my food isn't warming in the oven like I've told her time and time again. Dread builds in my gut at the thought of what I have to do. Again. I feel like a father on one of those old shows who used to say, "This is going to hurt me more than it hurts you." Every time I think about getting help for my temper, Donovan calls me a pussy and I change my mind. I hate hurting her, but fuck, it's the only way she seems to learn anything.

"Fuck." I slam the oven door so hard that the glass cracks and the spices lined up on the back tumble over, crashing to the counter and floor below.

"She's making fun of you, you know. What else can it be? You told her and told her. She won't learn unless you show her you mean business." Donovan grabs my cigarette from my fingers, taking a puff. He blows on the tip, giving me a wink as he hands it back. "You know what to do." He takes the other muffin off the plate and walks out the door. I hear the front door close behind him before I move.

I made her taste blood the last time she had the nerve to look in my face and defy me. My own blood stuttering in my veins, I throw my dinner plate at the wall, the steak on the floor now covered with shards of broken glass. Damn it. And damn her for making me crazy. *The whiskey slowing my thinking and throwing gasoline on my rage, I lick my lips and head for our bedroom.*

She's asleep on the bed, facedown. The bottle of sleeping pills she frequents lies on the nightstand. Rolling up my sleeves, I stride across the room in three long, pissed-off steps and climb on the bed. She barely moves when I mount her, positioning myself over top of her so she can't fight me. I have an easy hundred pounds on her, so there's no way she can move me off her.

I push up the T-shirt and look down at the smooth bronze skin of my wife's back. My Brooklyn. The lit weapon dangles between my fingers as I hesitate.

She screams when I press the fire into her skin, squirming and bucking under me.

"Cain! Please! I'm sorry!" she sobs.

I pull the cigarette away, sneering at the perfect black circle it left behind. "You don't ever listen, do you? I'm so sick of repeating myself."

"What did I—"

I press it to her skin again. Another scream that chills my blood, her tears soaking the pillow.

She won't forget this time.

***

I wake covered in sweat, my whole body shaking. Donavan smiles at me, grinning from ear to ear. His dark hair framing his eyes, he sits on the cheap hotel bed beside me, a bottle of whiskey pressed to his lips as he laughs at me.

"Pleasant dreams?"

I know I talk in my sleep, so his mocking laugh is nothing new. I rub my face with a guttural groan, shaking the dream/memory off.

"I hate you." I really do hate him for what he made me into. This monster, this… beast. I was a normal kid with a normal temper. I'd never even been in a fight until he came along, starting shit with all his whispers in my ear.

He laughs, a deep, rolling sound I know all too well. "Good. I'd worry if you loved me."

"You know what I mean." I sit up, shaking off the dream/memory and glancing out the window. Daylight filters through the curtains, casting beams here and there across the room. I wonder what time it is, how long I slept. "I never would've hurt her if not for you."

He nods. "Yes, yes, I know. The lovesick little puppy." He scoffs. "I made you a man," he seethes in my face, his gaze penetrating. "You were going to end up a weak-ass mama's boy if I hadn't come along."

I look away. That's probably true. But Brooklyn always liked me before she saw my temper. I see the phone in his hand and can't stop the question, knowing what I know about him and his knack for finding trouble.

"Where is she?"

"Your mom knows."

"You called my mom?" I ask over my shoulder, heading for the bathroom. I piss with the door open, waiting for his bullshit response.

"No, but I know she knows." He laughs. "I don't know where she is. I'm not God, for fuck's sake. Like I'm omniscient."

"Omniscient? Is that another word for stupid asshole?" I flush the toilet. "You're useless. How do you know if you didn't call her?"

"I have my ways. Call your mom." He never tells me how he knows shit like that, and I don't know why. He tosses the phone and it bounces on my bed.

My mom. Another love-hate relationship. Sure, she fed me and gave me a roof, but after my dad left, she was less the warm, caring mother and more the man-hungry, constantly drinking slut. So now, eighteen years later, she's much older than her years and used up.

"How does she know anything?"

"Who knows, but she has your money. With that, you can do what you need to find her."

I stand there in the hotel room, looking at Donovan as he leans on the headboard, taking a drag of a cigarette and watching me.

I laugh, running a hand over my face. *Dear old Mom.*

Crossing the room in a few short strides, I pick up the phone and dial her number, not wasting time with pleasantries when she answers on the second ring.

"Mom, it's me. I'm out."

"How are you, son? Did you do all right?"

I roll my eyes. Did I do all right? What a stupid thing to ask, as if I went to Vegas or something.

"I'm fine. I'm a big, mean son of a bitch. You should know that, considering you made me this way. You and… well, never mind. I need two things."

"Let me guess."

She agrees to meet me at the Waffle House in town to give me the account number for my money. Money I inherited, money Brook never knew about and I had Mom keep from me back then. My drinking and gambling weren't good for an account with half a million dollars in it.

Dear old Dad, he was good for something besides leaving after all. Not to mention Donovan, who talked me into stashing it instead of drinking and gambling it away or spending it on whores. For once, he was useful.

***

I stuff a bite of waffles in my mouth and wash it down with black coffee. "You look like hell."

Mom glares at me, sipping her own coffee. Her red

hair matches mine, but now it's frizzy and laced with gray, piled in a messy bun that looks slept on. Her cloudy blue eyes are bloodshot. "You don't look too hot either, son. You said—"

I nod. "I know. I'll bring you the money later. Thanks for taking care of it. I'll give you the $20,000 I promised. Now tell me you know where my wife is."

"I want more money."

Taking a deep breath, I set down my fork and cross my arms over my chest. Should've seen this coming. Controlling myself in this crowded diner is my first priority. Not reaching across the table and dragging her out of here by her hair is the second.

I glance at Donovan, who's sitting beside me, and smirk. He pats me on the back with a grin. It was his idea to promise her the money. Me actually paying out is another matter entirely. We'll see what happens.

My jaw set, I look across the table. My glare shuts her up quick. She knows I'm not above hitting her. "I'll pay you, but not until I find her. Got it?"

She nods, light returning to her eyes. "I want another ten. That money should be mine, but the bastard hid it from me."

"He hid it from everyone. He stole it, remember? Who cares? Now talk."

Out of the corner of my eye, I see Donovan lean back in the booth, watching silently with his arms crossed over his chest.

"After she left and you got arrested, she called me.

She wanted money. I had nothing to offer her, but I said she could stay with me, at least. She'd been in and out of shelters, having to leave because they all wanted to get the police involved, who would call Child Protective Services." She pauses as the waitress freshens her coffee, then takes her time stirring sugar into it before she goes on.

"Having no way to care for Carissa, she would run. Soon enough, she ran out of places to go and ended up on the streets. That's when I heard from her. I had nothing to give her, and she refused to let me take them in. I'm sure she knew that if I got my hands on Carissa, she'd probably never see her again, so she turned me down. Periodically I'd give her twenty bucks or so, but that's all I had. She'd come by and shower and get a meal occasionally, but she never let the kid out of her sight." After another slow sip of coffee, she eyes me over the cup before she goes on.

"I heard she got rescued by the people she works for now. They gave her money and means to get back on her feet. Once she didn't need me anymore, I told her if she didn't let me see Carissa once a month, I'd call the cops and tell them everything. I think she doubted that the cops would care, but she wasn't willing to risk it. She's missed the last couple of months though, puts it off with excuses."

I lean forward, my heart pounding. The taste of coffee in my mouth makes my rising nausea worse. *They lived on the streets? My wife and child?* "How long did they live out there?" I try to steady my voice, but it still comes out with gravel in it.

Her eyes widen a bit, and she takes in a short breath. "Six months? Maybe eight. Not too long."

"Not too long." The words echo over and over as my blood rushes in my ears like a train, and bile touches the back of my tongue.

On.

The.

Streets.

My family.

I lean over the table, right in her face. "You're telling me that my wife, the love of my life, and my daughter lived on the streets? Homeless? For eight months?"

She must be joking.

"Yes. You heard what I said. She ran out of means for support and refused to report you because she didn't want to lose the baby."

The realization that it's my fault pushes down the nausea, gagging me. I stuck that gun in her face. I scared her, and she ran. If she'd reported me, I'd still be in prison, but she would've lost Carissa. My daughter might've ended up in foster care, or with my mother. *But she almost did end up with my mom when I was going to kill us both. What was I thinking, assuming Carissa would be okay with her? This useless woman?*

God, what did I do?

A weight falls on me, pinning me down, one I've never felt before.

Regret.

It wraps around my heart like icy steel fingers and squeezes until I can't breathe. My lungs won't expand; I can't catch my breath. She sits across the table from me, staring at me like a moron, completely clueless to what's happening within me right now.

Brooklyn was safe, warm, and fed under my roof—well, as safe as anyone could be living with me. But the streets? Rape, murder, hunger, cold, weather, perverts eyeballing my baby girl. I can imagine what Brook might've had to do to keep her safe. *If* she kept her safe.

Fuck, I can't breathe.

My heart starts beating again, but out of rhythm, and I realize as the sweat breaks out on my forehead that I'm having a panic attack. I close my eyes and breathe as deeply as my lungs will let me, trying to stave it off, to calm myself down before I erupt.

"Are they safe? Is my daughter safe?" I ask, my voice thick.

"Yes, she's fine now."

I have so many questions, but I can't ask them because if I don't like the answer, I'll jump over this table and hurt the woman who gave me life.

If anyone deserves it, it's her, but for the first time I find myself thinking about the consequences of my rage, this blackness that Donovan sends me into with his whispered taunts and words of "wisdom," making me see things I might not otherwise have before.

Taking my mom's hand, I look into her hard, overly made-up face. "You think that's not a long time? You let my family live out there and did nothing but toss her a twenty? Do you know what could've happened to them?"

"I couldn't. She wouldn't let me—"

I squeeze her hand hard, grinding the knuckles together until tears form in her eyes. She knows better than to cry out, alerting anyone to our little entanglement. "You had money. *My* money. One phone call and I would've taken care of her. That's all it would've taken, and you know it, you selfish bitch."

"Please, you're hurting me!"

I lean forward even more. "I know."

"You hid the money from her. I didn't think—"

"You're right, you didn't. Now be a good mommy and tell me where she is. Is she still in Dallas?"

She nods, trying to pull her hand away. I grip it tighter. "Yes, she lives in an apartment. Works at The Blue Room. It's a club downtown."

I finally let her hand go, and she jerks it away from me. "Write down the address or you get nothing."

Crying, my mom drops her injured hand to her lap and rushes to get a pen out of her purse with the other. I reach across Donovan for a napkin, and he nods proudly.

Chapter Three

BROOKLYN

PRESENT DAY

IT'S THAT EVENING WHEN MY PHONE rings. The phone call that I didn't know would change everything, yet still the one I've been preparing for all this time. After dropping off my daughter and parking my car, I walk into the empty, closed club, pulling the ringing cell out of my purse to answer.

"Hello."

"Is this Brooklyn James?"

"Who is this?"

I can't make out the noise in the background on the line, wondering if it's just a bad connection or if she's really somewhere that loud. "My name is Mary, and I'm with the Texas Department of Criminal Justice. I'm calling to advise you that your husband has been released from custody."

The world sways around me, and I wonder if I heard her correctly. I swallow even though my mouth is dry, choking out a reply as I grip the rail on the bar next to me, steadying myself. "What?"

"He was released three days ago." She says it as if it's nothing. As if she might not have just destroyed my life. *He's been out for three days?* But why is she calling? It doesn't even make sense.

"Why are you notifying me? He wasn't arrested for assaulting me. You guys don't do that for DWI, do you?"

"Yes, I understand that, and no ma'am, we don't. When his file was being processed, there was a request that you be notified. I apologize for the delay, but we've been short-staffed here due to budget cuts."

I sit on a barstool, glancing around to make sure no one else is here. What if a vendor is walking around? Or the bartender came in early and I didn't notice his car in the parking lot? I've worked hard to keep this part of my life in the shadows, away from almost everyone. "Can you tell me who made the request?"

"I'm afraid not. We can't release that information, I'm sorry."

I blow out a breath, having figured as much. But you never know when you'll get that one person who will bend the rules, or simply doesn't know the rules. "Um, okay then. Thanks, Mary." What else do I say? Thanks for destroying my life?

"You're welcome, ma'am. Have a nice evening."

The conversation ends, and I put the phone back in my purse without thinking. I've told myself that I would know what to do when this happened. I've had a mental checklist for close to two years now.

Call Ashley and let her know.

Call the school.

Consider changing my name, my daughter's name.

No, scratch that. I won't run. I won't hide. I've been training, and I've been shooting; I know how to handle the gun, and myself. I'm strong now. I can do this. I have to. Because he *will* show up. He *will* find me.

I have no doubt.

Taking a deep, shaky breath, I shoulder my purse and walk through the main area, hoping to lose myself in my work, even for a short while. Preferring distraction to fear, I head down the hall. My office is at the end, with my boss occupying my doorway. Shane leans against the jamb with a laugh floating in his eyes as a loud thump sounds nearby. I see the hind end of a nicely filled-out pair of jeans sticking out from under my desk, then hear a masculine grumble.

"Motherfucker." The word is muffled, followed by another thump. "*Puto escritorio,*" he groans in Spanish, and I glance at Shane, who simply laughs again.

"You know," the muffled voice floats out, "I'm not an IT guy. I write software, not install hardware. This isn't my job."

"I know. You've told me that like seven times now, but you're doing a friend a favor, remember?"

"Favor? No, I'm getting paid for this. I can't believe I let you talk me into this." He manages to connect whatever it is he's been struggling with in the cramped, dark space, then crawls out, rubbing his head. "And now I have a headache."

Recognition lights my brain up as I watch the stranger stop while still on his knees and look at me. His bright, smiling eyes gaze into mine. This guy, whoever he is, I've seen him in the club many times, usually watching me with an intensity that makes me flush. No man has ever looked at me the way he has. Even Cain never did.

My pulse thumps as I watch the handsome stranger rub his fingers over a head of dark blond hair, sun-kissed forearms accenting his muscles with every move he makes. He climbs off the floor and parks himself in my chair before rolling up to the desk, taking control of the keyboard. I chastise myself for my reaction to the man, knowing this is *not* the time.

"So, this is your computer guy?" I finally ask.

My face heats when the stranger leans back in the chair, staring boldly at me. His eyes glide rapidly over me, only to settle back on my face, my eyes. My stomach flutters, but I steel my emotions so they won't show. Even so, I can't seem to look away from him, hating myself the whole time. I just got the call that I've been dreading for years, and now I'm all stupid because of a cute stranger.

Fucking men.

"This is Brandon. Brandon, this is my manager, Brooklyn. This is her office."

"Hi, Brooklyn." His voice wraps around my name, and I suck in a breath. I finally tear my eyes away and look down at my old Reeboks, trying to compose myself, remembering what all I've been through. The memories are like cold water on any fire that man might've sparked. *Fuck no.*

"Sorry about my language. I didn't know you were there. Hey, I've seen you before." His voice is deep and smooth and draws my eyes up. He sits lazily in the chair, legs spread wide. My eyes are drawn to muscled thighs, tracing his shape as I wonder how tall he is when he stands.

I finally find my voice. "I've seen you too, in the club some nights."

"You never said hello." His grin lights up his whole face and causes a stutter in my chest that I don't appreciate.

"Neither did you." I raise an eyebrow at him. As if challenged, his smile grows broader. He eyes me as he rolls closer to the desk, turning his hypnotic hazel eyes to the computer.

I look at Shane. "What's he doing?"

Shane crosses his arms, covered from shoulder to wrist in tattoo sleeves that are exposed by his T-shirt. "I told you about this upgrade."

"I thought that was only for the point-of-sale stuff."

"No, it's everything. He already installed the point-of-sale, but he needs to train you so you both can train the staff this evening."

Great. More time with this guy.

I glance at him, but he's focused on the computer screen.

"All right then. I guess I'll leave you two and go make my rounds. I'll do the office work later." I start to turn when Brandon's voice stops me.

"See you in a bit, Brooklyn." I hear the grin, the way he stresses my name, but I refuse to turn. If I do, he'll see my smile, and I can't have that. I can't have anything right now.

I don't answer, just walk out, my guts in my shoes.

***

"The tablets are connected to the register, so the waitstaff won't have to come to the bar to close out tabs now," he continues. A box of preprogrammed tablets sits on the floor, one for each of the staff and a second box of extras.

I touch the icons on the tablet in front of me as directed, hyperaware of Brandon standing over my shoulder at the bar downstairs. He smells like Acqua di Giò, a cologne I've always liked. His scent drifts over to me, tickling my senses and drawing me closer to him. My body language screams one thing, but my brain's screaming another, and that's the one I need to listen to.

"This seems really easy to use." I look up to find him staring at me.

He watches my eyes, a light smile dancing in his hazel ones. "It is. They won't have any trouble."

"So, you write software? How come you're doing this?" I gesture toward the boxes.

He sighs. "A favor. The owners are friends with my daughter's mother. I was talked into it."

"You have a daughter?"

"Yeah. She's almost four. We share custody. I have her every other week."

"I have a five-year-old girl myself. I guess that must be why I don't see you in here every Saturday night?"

"Yeah, I don't go out like I used to before. So, why didn't you ever say hello to me?"

I laugh at his boldness, feeling that flush all over again. *What to say?* I glance up, finding him leaning on the bar, eyes down.

"I'm working. I don't have much time to socialize, you know? It's a busy place."

He nods. "That's true. Are you single?" His eyes fall to my bare ring finger.

"Yes."

"Good."

I laugh again, shaking my head. "Don't get any ideas."

He grins at me, giving me a sideways look.

"Looks like your staff is showing up."

He nods toward the door, where three waitresses are fluttering in an hour before their shift starts. One of the bartenders is behind them.

Thank God, a distraction.

After the meeting, we open the club, and it seems that no one will be having any issues with the new equipment. They all love it. Just as they scatter and I'm watching Brandon bend to pick up one of the two boxes we need to carry back upstairs, my cell phone rings.

I grab it, glancing to see that it's a number I don't recognize. "Hello."

No answer, just dead air. I pull the phone away and look at it, thinking the caller hung up, but the line is still open. When I place it back to my ear, I hear distinct breathing. My blood thickens. The room dims around me, and I stumble, falling to a barstool just a foot or so behind me, gripping the bar tightly.

"Hello? Who is this?" I try to sound commanding, but it comes out squeaky. Maybe it's not anyone. Maybe it's a wrong number. Besides, how could he get my number so fast?

Of course, then it dawns on me. His mother. Damn me for being stupid. For wanting some kind of family for Carissa, even if it was just that woman. But then with all those threats, I was worried she might really go through with it and something might happen. Even on the crazy, slim chance that it might be possible, I couldn't risk it.

I hang up after another beat or two of my heart in my ears, blood drained from my face. Setting the phone on the bar, I look up and see Brandon is watching with concern, the larger of the two boxes of hardware in his arms.

It occurs to me that the next corner I turn, Cain might be standing there. I swallow my tears, refusing to allow the panic to take over. I can't. I can't, not this time.

"You okay?" Brandon steps toward me.

No, not even a little bit. "I'm fine. Just some bad news," I mumble, turning and bending to pick up the other, smaller box with trembling hands. "Follow me to the elevator. We can take this stuff back to my office."

Chapter Four

CAIN

Twenty-Four Hours Ago

"YOU THINK HE MIGHT GIVE ME THE JOB back? After prison?" I ask, checking my reflection in the glass of the high-rise where I used to work. I was the best IT guy Griffin Software Solutions ever had.

Since I was released, I got a new suit, haircut, the works. Not that I give a shit about this job, or even need it right now. However, if I'm going to make a decent impression on my wife and heal my marriage, having a job is going to matter. Women don't respect men who don't work. And it's all about respect. It was nice to work, however. Something that came so easily to me that I could do it without thinking, or be hungover and it wouldn't matter.

My stomach still roils at the thought of what my mother told me. Homeless. Since I found out yesterday that they'd been living on the streets for months, I haven't been able to think about anything else. My sick imagination is doing horrible things to me, thinking about what could've happened to them, and Donovan doesn't help.

I know I went too far, pushing her to something so drastic. This is my first step to fixing it, and Donovan doesn't need to know. As far as he believes, Brooklyn is mine, like I possess her, and I need to reclaim my property. Mere hours ago, I pretty much agreed with him, my love for her making me crazy.

Donovan stands with an arm around me, hissing in my ear. "It was a DWI, man. It's forgivable."

"What about the assault?"

He shrugs as he takes a seat on a bench, stretching his long jean-clad legs out, forcing a woman to walk around him when she passes us. He winks at her, but she just glances at me and then walks on without a word. "It was tossed out, remember? He won't know you were almost busted for knocking that guy's teeth in. Just go. Stop whining."

I nod, psyching myself up to open the door and head up to the seventh floor where the office is. Where my old boss, Brandon, is. He was a decent guy, and as far as he ever knew, I was a decent guy too. Here's hoping charm overrides sense.

Onward and upward.

As I ride the elevator, preparing my bullshit speech and perfecting my smile, I laugh at myself, unable to believe I'm walking through these doors once again. I never imagined myself back here. Being arrested probably saved my life. I might've ended it. But here I am, back to do the one thing I could be good at without thinking about it, without really trying. Computers don't have smart mouths to piss me off, smiles and curves to tempt me. Just cold hardware, a distraction from my personal hell for eight hours a day. I almost liked it. Almost. When the doors open, I'm greeted with the same old lobby from three years ago, just filled with new furniture—buttery leather and dark wood—and a different receptionist. Some guy sits behind the counter now, glancing up at me with an instant fake grin and chirpy attitude. "Welcome to Griffin Software Solutions. May I help you?"

I go into an overly cheerful explanation that I used to work here, and I'd like to speak with Brandon Maradona. He takes my name and offers me a coffee while I wait, which I accept.

Soon enough, Brandon comes around the corner and into the lobby. Tall, a little over thirty, blond. Smart and rich is what this guy is.

Once in his office, after all the small talk, we get down to the point of my visit. "So, Mr. Maradona, I had a bit of bad luck, of my own doing unfortunately. I was wondering what the odds are of coming back to work here?"

He leans back in his chair, seeming to study me, thinking on what I'm asking him. I know I have about a 50/50 shot, so I'll need to play my cards right. "DWI, right?"

I nod. "Yeah. I took classes in jail. I can produce documents if you like."

"Cain, you were a damn good IT guy. It would be nice to have you back on the team, but I have to ask my boss."

"I understand. I liked working here, and honestly, three years in jail gave me some time to think and straighten out some bad habits."

He nods. "Sit tight. I'll be back in a few minutes."

My pulse pounds out a hopeful beat. Ten minutes goes by before he finally returns.

"Cain, if you can produce the documents showing you took the classes, we're okay with giving you a probationary return. You understand that, right?"

I nod, standing and extending my hand to shake his. "Yes, of course. I'm not drinking anymore, so it won't be an issue. Thank you. I appreciate this."

And just like that, I'm back in. My old job, money in my pocket.

Only one thing missing.

***

BROOKLYN

Present Day

I press the button as I take a deep breath, glancing back. "You can just leave the box here if you need to go. I can manage."

"I don't mind."

My heart starts to pound as the bell dings and the doors open; my palms sweat, my stomach shrinking into a hard, sick knot. "I hate these things," I mutter, forcing a deep breath in and out as I step inside. I fold myself into the corner after hitting the button. My heart stutters when the door closes and the room shrinks.

"What, elevators?"

Closing my eyes, I nod. Maybe if I keep them closed for the short ride, I'll be able to breathe.

"Yes."

"Then why not take the stairs?"

"Because once I was a person who let fear control me, and I refuse to do it again, no matter how much I hate it." Taking deep breaths, I finally open my eyes and look up, head against the wall. His eyes are on me, full of both concern and confusion.

Just as he opens his mouth to speak, there's a sick grinding sound, and the elevator car lurches before coming to a stop. For a second, I stop breathing. He sets the box down, then moves to the panel. "We stopped."

My breathing comes in short, shallow bursts as I watch him push buttons, nothing happening. He pushes the Call button, but again there's nothing.

"We're stuck."

"What?" My eyes widen as I try to back farther into the wall. "Are you sure?" I set the box down and pat my pockets. No phone. "I left my phone on the bar," I groan.

He does the same. "Shit, mine's on your desk." He meets my eyes and takes a step toward me. "Hey, we'll be just fine. Just don't panic. Breathe with me."

Just to have something to focus on, I stare up at him, trying to forget.

Don't think about the dark. Don't think about that unseen critter that just crawled across your bare foot and up your leg. Or the hunger, or the hours and hours in the dark. Banging on the closet door from the inside, begging when I know there isn't anyone to hear me.

But I can't not think about it, and in a flash, I'm there again.

* * *

I'm shaking, having seen the darkness in his eyes before. He smells of cigarettes and whiskey and sweat when he jerks me roughly to my feet, pressing me against his body. His words come out in a low, hissing growl. "You think you can just do what you want? Come and go without asking me?"

I shake my head. "No, no, I don't think so. I just thought—"

"You thought you could get a job and hide money from me? I provide for you, end of story." Spit flies off his lips and lands on my face. I make no move to wipe it away.

"I'm sorry, Cain. I thought it would help. I just wanted to pay the bills, I swear. I'd never leave you," I lie. It's all I think about, but finding out I was pregnant last week stopped me. I haven't even told him yet.

"You saying I can't cut it?" He pushes me away, hard. I stumble, landing roughly on the floor. He starts pacing, and I don't know if I should get up or stay down, play dead—as if he's a pissed-off rabid bear and sniffing me will suffice. I wish.

"No. I don't mean—"

He moves quickly, jerking me to my feet and dragging me down the hall as I beg, trying to keep up without falling down.

"Sit in here until I think you've learned." I stand in stunned disbelief as he opens the hall closet door. He pulls out a few boxes, making room, and then shoves me inside, slamming the door.

Darkness swallows me, except for the light under the door. I don't dare try the knob; I'm not that stupid. Minutes pass, and then I hear footsteps, followed by banging that shakes the door. I reach up blindly, feeling around until I prick myself on a nail that's come through the wood. He's nailed me in.

I take a deep breath, but my lungs won't expand. I fall back into coats, caught by a box of something *that crunches under my weight as I gasp, hands on the walls of the small space.*

"Cain?" I call out meekly. "Cain?"

"Not a word," he orders through the door before fading footsteps tell me he's walked off.

* * *

I was in that closet for two days. Peeing on myself, begging for water, falling asleep only to jerk awake and find myself confused and terrified. When he finally opened the door, the light flooded in and hurt my eyes. He had a bubble bath ready for me. He gently washed me, telling me he was sorry. He fed me, brushed my hair even. Told me he loved me, and I believed him. I was a fool. Hopeful because of the baby I carried, that it might change him. That it might protect me.

But that's not where I am. It's been years, and I'm not locked in the closet as punishment from the man I married. I'm here.

So I take in a breath, breathing with Brandon, looking up into clearly worried eyes, hoping and praying I don't have some kind of a flashback. I blink away tears before my gaze darts away from him, ashamed of my emotions. Will I always be crippled by some form of fear? Some secret terror that threatens to take everything from me?

No. For my child, I refuse. I wipe the tears, take a

slow, deep breath into my lungs, and blow it out.

"It's going to be okay," he says again.

"Okay, breathe, Brooklyn. Just breathe," I tell myself, closing my eyes.

"Someone will miss us. Just focus on me and try not to think about whatever you have going on in your head right now."

All I can do is nod and slink down the wall, holding my knees and tucking my head between them, closing my eyes against the darkness of the closet in my mind.

"Tell me about yourself." His deep voice touches my ears. "We might as well talk about something, right?"

Looking up, I wipe the dampness from my eyelashes with shaking hands. "You go first."

He sits, stretching out long legs, cocking his head to one side with a hint of a smile. I avoid his eyes, looking anywhere but at his face, his gaze.

"Okay. My name is Brandon Maradona. I'm thirty-three years old, single, and I'm a software architect. I've worked for Griffin Software Solutions for six years, and I already told you about my daughter. "

Griffin Software. An alarm goes off in my head, like a tiny fire truck driving in circles, screaming at me to pay attention. Cain worked for Griffin Software as an IT tech. *Did Brandon know him?* I never met anyone he worked with, so he wouldn't know me. "You work for Griffin Software?"

He gives me a slow nod. "Is that not okay?"

"No, it's fine. I just confused them with someone else." I hug my knees tighter. What a small world. It's been too long for me to remember the names of anyone Cain might've mentioned back then, people he worked with, worked for. Maybe this guy worked in a different department and has never met Cain. I need to stop freaking out over every little thing.

"So, what about you? Tell me about yourself."

"Brooklyn James. I have a five-year-old, Carissa. Ashley, Shane's wife, watches her for me when I'm working. I work ten-hour shifts four days a week, around the weekends."

"How long have you worked here?"

"About three years. I started as a waitress, then worked my way up. How is it that you speak Spanish? You look white to me."

"My mom is from Spain, raised us bilingual. I have a twin brother too. He has a couple of kids. My dad took off when we were really small, so she raised us alone."

"Never remarried?"

"Nope."

"Are you fluent?"

His smile makes me laugh, though I don't even know why. It's like a little boy who knows he's about to get into trouble but doesn't care. "*Sí, eres tan inquisitivo como bello.*"

I pick up a couple of words: inquisitive, beautiful. Smiling, I relax my grip on my legs and laugh at him.

"Does that usually work for you?"

"What?"

"Flirting in Spanish."

He laughs, meeting my eyes. "You speak Spanish?"

"No, not really. Just a word here and there." I shake my head. "Is that what you do? Be all cute and charming in Spanish to lure women?"

"I'm cute and charming in English too."

"So you say."

"You said it, not me."

"That's not what I said—"

"It's okay, beautiful, you don't have to be shy."

I raise an eyebrow, relaxing my legs. "I'm not shy."

"Good, because I love spicy women."

I roll my eyes at him, and he chuckles. It's in that moment that I realize he managed to do it. He saved me from myself. I forgot to be scared, wasn't locked in the closet in my head. Some form of gratitude or peace, I don't know which, washes over me as I'm able to breathe freely without freaking out in a confined space for the first time in ages. Forcing myself to do it never did anything but send me into a nauseated cold sweat anyway. Now, meeting his warm eyes, I'm okay.

I wonder what that means. Probably nothing. Just a distraction, that's all. He's probably good with people, charming.

"What happened with her mom? Your daughter, I mean."

"What a question. Well, long story short, I screwed up.

I waited too late to realize it, and that's that."

"What did you do?" I sit cross-legged, trying to relax in the small space as he crosses his legs at the ankles.

"Well, we had a thing that lasted a few months. I got a job offer in Seattle, and I took it and moved because I was starting to feel some things for her and it scared me. I'd never been committed to anyone, never really wanted to be, and my feelings freaked me out. The job was a way out of my own feelings, or so I thought. While I was gone, she called and told me she was pregnant. I realized I was a moron and moved back, but by the time I did, she was with someone else. I lost her 'cause I dragged my feet, and it bit me in the ass."

Silence falls for a moment, but then he tosses out the question I knew would come eventually. "What about yours, the father?"

Chapter Five

BROOKLYN

NOW I'M FACED WITH IT. THE QUESTION I always hate, embarrassed of the answer. I swallow once more and steel my emotions, masking my face as best I can. "Well, he went to jail for DWI. What's that tell you?"

"That it wasn't his first rodeo."

I nod. "Exactly. He had a problem. He had lots of problems. So I left."

He cocks his gorgeous head to one side; a smile tickles his lips. My stomach flutters under the scrutiny of his bright eyes.

I look away. "He seemed decent—*seemed* being the operative word there." I let out a laugh, not because it's funny but because it's all so damn ironic. What if this guy used to work with Cain? I have no idea in what capacity, but he might have. Maybe he knew him. Though he might not even remember him, if there is anything to remember.

"Sounds like you've been through some stuff."

"Everyone's been through stuff."

"No shit, Sherlock. Of course everyone has, but you're clearly hiding something." He laughs at me when I glare at him, surprised and a little pissed that he called me out when we don't even know each other.

"Look, just because we're stuck in here doesn't make us best friends."

My answer is simple enough, but for some reason his eyes glitter as if he's won something. I watch him lick his lips and struggle to wipe the grin off his face.

What's it like to be so happy that you're smiling all the time? I live with fear, and PTSD, and nightmares. Looking over my shoulder, praying Cain doesn't show up—it's endless. I can't imagine that kind of peace.

But one thing I refuse to do is run. I won't run this time.

"Well, regardless, he's out of jail. They called me earlier." I sound way more nonchalant than I feel. And that was before the second call. I'm nauseated knowing he's out there.

"Will he look for you?"

"I'd be surprised if he didn't."

"What will you do?"

"What do you mean?"

"If he shows up. What will you do?"

Get my gun, scream my head off, be ready to kill if I have to. "I don't know. I hope he doesn't. I just want him to leave me alone. He's done enough damage."

Brandon nods, shifting on the uncomfortable floor. "I'm sorry you had to deal with that. Being married to an alcoholic must've been awful. But people can change, right? What if he realized the error of his ways or something?"

At that, I look straight into Brandon's eyes, bolstered by my anger toward Cain and everything I endured at his hand. "You have no idea what he did to me. No amount of Jesus or pretty promises can ever undo what that son of a bitch did." My whisper is almost a growl. I meant to lie, I really did. I had every intention of crafting a story about what happened to my child's father, something simple, but here I am spewing the truth at this man I just met. To be quite honest, it feels good to share it with someone. The first people I ever told were Ashley and Shane. It's because of them that I made it this far, got off the streets and kept my daughter by my side. It was easy to trust them then, and they're like family now. Telling someone new seems foreign, almost wrong, yet here I am. I guess after all this time, maybe it's my brain's way of telling me to stop hiding, that maybe I shouldn't be so afraid, so ashamed.

Brandon cocks his head to one side. "So tell me. I'm a good listener."

My heart thumps. He rests his head on the wall but keeps his eyes on me, patience and understanding personified.

Do I tell him? Do I confess that I spent years getting

almost killed over and over again, only to come back to more?

"Do the details matter that much?"

"I'm sure they do to you."

"Why do you want to know?"

"Because you're scared to tell me."

His honesty is a bit jarring and throws me off my game of eluding him.

He thinks I'm scared?

Well, I am scared. I live and breathe terror.

Stunned to silence, I just stare at him until the pounding in my chest becomes distracting and I have to look away.

"Let me guess. Did he cheat on you?"

I nod.

"More than once?"

"More than a dozen, probably."

His smile fades. "He did something worse, didn't he? I can see it in your eyes."

Why are we even talking about this? Why does it have to be about me and my past? Why is he so curious? I glance over at him. Why is he so damn handsome? So casual and yet concerned. And why is he looking at me like that? Soft curiosity and attraction all over him, and he isn't trying to hide it. And why in the hell am I telling him?

Maybe I just need to be free of the lies. Ashley told me to be proud of what I am, proud of my strength. But I know the poor, pathetic looks I'd get if people knew.

The whispers after I walk away of "Why would she stay?" and "Maybe she deserved it" that they wouldn't dare say to my face. But I'm so sick of pretending to be someone else.

"He did horrible things to me." My voice cracks.

"He hurt you, didn't he?" His smile is gone now, something dark replacing the light that was dancing in his eyes just moments ago. He knows. He's too smart not to have put it together by now. "Why didn't you reach out?"

"I was scared and confused, and just stupid. He almost killed me, Brandon. He's not just some asshole who was a shitty husband. He's a monster."

The weight of my confession looms between us in this small space, making it feel even smaller. But somehow, Brandon proves a distraction from it. I focus on him and our conversation, and the fear seems to be just a little less.

"Is he the reason for your claustrophobia?"

I nod slowly, and his brow furrows. "What did he do?"

"Enough."

The details don't matter, not anymore. To lay all that out would be to focus on the wrong thing. Besides, I don't need to drag one more mind into the sickness that is my memories.

Brandon seems to understand, and no further questions come.

I watch him stand up and step over the boxes, moving

toward me. He sits beside me, turning sideways so he can see my face. The closeness of him makes me take in a deep breath, hoping he doesn't notice it. When he grabs my hand, the air sticks in my lungs as his large hand wraps around mine, heat and electricity sending sparks coursing throughout my body. Like times past, I can't stop my eyes from moving up to meet his, finding him watching me with that same intense stare I've caught before.

"I'm sorry. I wish I had known you back then."

"Why?"

"Because I would've never let it happen."

Something in his tone tells me he means it. I swallow hard and bite back the sarcasm that bubbles up automatically.

"You don't even know me." My voice is a whisper.

"I know enough."

I want to look away, but I can't.

He leans in, as if to press his next words into me. "I know you're a mom who would do anything for her daughter. I know you do what you have to. I know you won't let fear take you down. I know you work hard and that you don't like attention. I know you're one of the most beautiful creatures I've ever seen."

I cock my head to one side. "Are you trying to seduce me?"

His smile is slow, then turns into a grin that I can't help but laugh at.

"No, if I were trying to seduce you, I might do this."

He turns my hand and presses hot lips to the inside of my wrist. I'd pull away, but it feels too damn good. His soft, swift kiss speaks to the deepest, hungriest parts of me, parts that haven't been awakened in years, and it shocks me that something so small can change that. I thought those desires long gone, tortured away night after night.

I guess I was wrong.

"Or this." He leans in, lips all but touching my ear as his voice turns into a silky whisper. "*O podría susurrar algo sexy, como este.*"

My Spanish isn't good enough to pick up everything he said, but a chill runs down my spine just the same.

"But I'm not doing that. We're just talking." He smiles, leaning back against the wall.

I shake my head, rolling my eyes at him when he laughs, his tongue flicking across his lips.

This man does something that no one else has ever been able to do before. He distracts me from my demons, my fear, and pulls me out of my own head.

I'm not sure if that's good or bad at this point, but it feels good to be thinking about something else for a change.

***

CAIN

I probably shouldn't be here so soon out of jail, but she has to know I'm sorry. By now, she must've forgiven me, but that last look she gave me, the one I remember that was blurred by the alcohol as I hid the gun from my kid, it haunts me still. Her eyes, resigned to death, yet still begging. The dark hope that swirled in them, the pleading on those lips, begging me to stop.

I would've pulled the trigger.

Now I sit here three years later in the parking lot of this club where my mom told me she works. Been sitting here for maybe half an hour in silence. I suck a drag out of my cigarette, the last one, and toss it out the window.

"What's the holdup?"

I look over into Donovan's cold face and know he won't understand. Whatever's wrong with me, it's worse in him. I know it, and he probably does too. I have anger and alcohol problems, but he's just nuts.

I grip the wheel. "What if she hates me?"

"She's your wife, so it doesn't matter."

"Maybe she's with someone else."

"You won't just sit and take that, will you? I taught you better than that, didn't I?"

I snort. "Taught me? You're not my dad."

"I'm the next best thing."

"You're not that much older than I am."

"It doesn't matter. I raised you. I taught you to be a man. Your mom sure didn't do that. I won't let you sit here and let this woman do this to you. Go in there and get your wife."

Sitting here isn't accomplishing anything, and I would like to see her again. I'm sure she's even more beautiful than I remember. That look flashes before me though. Cold eyes, her hair a crazy mess from me dragging her by it out of bed and into the bathroom. Her standing there, panting and weeping in the tub in just an old T-shirt, gun heavy in my hand and in her face. Cocked. Loaded.

She hated me. I deserved it.

But I love her.

I swear under my breath and get out of the car. Donovan doesn't follow me, and I leave him behind as I cross the parking lot, my heart pounding.

She's mine. The state of Texas says so. We aren't divorced. She never even reported me to the police, so that must mean something.

I show my ID to the bouncer at the door before I'm welcomed into the club. It's not busy, being a weeknight. I walk in, torn between the bar and walking around. Deciding I want to find her more than I want to drink, I search for employees, but seeing no one who can be her, I head up the stairs. The music is thumping through the overhead speakers, an empty stage to my right. It's probably occupied by a band on the weekends. A few people are dancing on the floor below while others sit on blue-and-white chairs, drinks in hand.

I don't see her. Maybe Mom was wrong. She said it had been a while since she talked to Brooklyn. Maybe she left and doesn't work here anymore.

A young, pretty redhead walks up to me, the bar logo emblazed across the chest of her uniform. "Hey, handsome, can I get you a drink?"

I look down at the petite woman, take in her ample chest, then look back up to her face and find her smiling at me.

One drink can't hurt.

"I'll take a whiskey. Say, do you know Brooklyn?"

She nods. "Oh, sure I do. She's my boss. How do you know her?"

She does work here. I smile, the first piece of the puzzle falling into place. "She's my wife. Can you tell me if she's here tonight?"

"Oh, well, she was here earlier. We had to come in early for training, but I haven't seen her in a while. She might've left."

I catch a hint of a strange look, one that wants to know why I don't know where my own wife is, and why she didn't know her boss was married. But she's a smart girl and doesn't ask, just smiles at me again.

It's a starting point, at least. She's close. I can almost feel her skin, smell her perfume. "Thanks... what's your name, beautiful?"

"Connie. I'll be right back with your drink."

Five-foot-nothing Connie bounces toward the bar, and I sit down in a white leather chair. Won't be long now. She'll forgive me. She has to—she loves me. No one can love her the way I do. She won't have forgotten that.

Chapter Six

BROOKLYN

I SIGH. "HOW LONG HAVE WE BEEN IN here?"

"Maybe an hour or two. I don't know."

"As much as I enjoy your company, I really want to get out of here." I stand up, walking in small circles to stretch my muscles. He moves his long legs, and I step over them.

"So, did you grow up here in Dallas?"

"Partly. I was born in California. We moved here when I was thirteen years old. I don't talk to my family now though. My parents stopped speaking to me when I left to get married, and then my sister died."

"Why did they—"

"I was barely eighteen, and he got me pregnant. I told them we were going to get married, and they told me that if I did, they wouldn't be around to pick me back up because he was 'bad news.' I ignored them, and we ran off together. I never saw them again. He wouldn't let me see my sister, but we talked on the phone." I pull a ponytail tie out of my pocket and put my hair into a loose knot on the back of my head.

"What happened to that baby?"

"He got drunk and kicked me in the stomach, though I told the hospital I fell. I had to give birth to a dead baby. I kicked him out, but he didn't leave, just slept on the front porch for days, crying and begging me to forgive him. Swore he'd never drink again. It was the first and last time I kicked him out, and he conned me into letting him back in. Thing is, I think he meant it at the time. He stopped drinking for a little bit, but it didn't last." It was a while ago, but I still look into my daughter's face and wonder if her brother would've looked like her, what he might be like. Shoving my hands into my pockets, I lean against the wall.

"You blame yourself, don't you?"

The question hits its mark, hard. I'm a bit shocked by the tears that fill my eyes, the pain that rips through me when I remember my son, carrying him, wondering if I could protect him or if he'd become a monster like his father. "My baby died. His name was Conner. I held him and buried him, and it's my fault because I let him hit me and I didn't leave. Then when I did finally decide to leave, my sister was killed in a car accident coming to get us."

I watch him stand slowly, not bothering to wipe my eyes or hide my tears this time. He closes in on me, and I think he's going to reach out for me, but he doesn't.

He just stands there looking pained, arms down at his sides.

"Don't do that. Please don't blame yourself."

"How can I not? The first time he hit me, I should've left. I was weak and stupid. I'll never not hate myself for it. Ever. God, why am I telling you all this?" I look down at my shoes. "People died because I was too afraid to leave him," I finish on a whisper.

I think he must agree, because the silence is so long, so pronounced.

"It's okay. You don't have to feel sorry for me. It's done. I'm—"

"It doesn't matter. It's over. You left. You and your daughter are safe. You're strong, so no, I don't feel sorry for you."

I look up to find an almost pissed-off expression on his face. "Then why are you looking at me like that?"

"Because I…." He groans. "I don't know, but I'm not standing here thinking less of you or whatever you're assuming. Everyone hurts. It's the strong ones who pull up and show the rest of us how pathetic we are for bitching about traffic lights or whatever else people whine about. Maybe people like you make people like me ashamed of ourselves."

I blink, taken aback by his confession. No one's ever put it to me like that before. No one's ever made me feel a sense of pride for what I am.

But it's fleeting. As fast as it comes, it dies, like a spark in a strong wind blown away. Too frail to hold its own.

In that moment, the door opens. Both our heads turn, and I see the top half of a pair of firemen who have pried it open. The elevator's partly between floors, but there's enough space for us to crawl through.

I meet Brandon's eyes once more before turning toward the door. After getting pulled out of the elevator, I'm separated from him. Frankly, I'm glad, but I know somehow it won't be the last I hear from him.

Shane sends me home, apologizing profusely for the elevator and for taking so long to notice that I wasn't on the floor working. Emotionally exhausted, I grab my things and leave without looking to see if Brandon is still around.

I just want to go home.

* * *

CAIN

After three drinks and no sign of Brook, I decide to leave. Being buzzed the first time she sees me since I got out probably isn't the best plan, so after one last hopeful search, I duck out and take off. I need to be on my best behavior when I see her and my daughter again, not like this. If I have any hope, I need to think clearly.

When I get back to the car, I don't know where Donovan is, but I leave anyway. He always manages to find his way no matter what. Lighting a cigarette, I don't get far before I find another bar, a small dive with a flashing neon light and no windows. I pull into the dark parking lot, lighting another cigarette as I leave the car and make my way inside.

Tomorrow is another day.

***

BROOKLYN

The next day, I wake up, run, lift, sweat, and work out harder than usual. I pack my gun, securing it in my car when I leave this time but hoping I won't have to use it. After I drop Carissa off, I head to work for another night.

I cross the parking lot, keys in hand, when I hear my name in a familiar voice. "Brooklyn, wait."

Stopping, I turn to face Brandon. He's in what looks like work clothes, a nice crisp button-down shirt and khakis. He walks toward me, away from a four-door black Dodge.

"What are you doing here?" I ask him. "We aren't open for a couple of hours."

Once close to me, his hands go into his pockets, and

he glances down at the concrete. "I know. I came to catch you. I couldn't find you last night after we got out of the elevator, and I wanted to ask if I can see you again."

See me again? After all the crap I told him? How can he want to see me again? "What?"

"I want to get your number."

"Why?" I can't stop the word from popping out of my flabbergasted mouth.

He smiles at me. "Because I like you, woman."

"You don't know me. I mean... I have so much baggage."

"I want to get to know you, and everyone has baggage."

I glance down at the concrete. I don't want a boyfriend. I don't want a man in my life, or love, or pain, of any of those other things that come with it. But this guy....

"Brandon, I—"

He steps closer, into my space, and I take in the scent of his cologne again. It's a warm smell that somehow comforts me.

"Brooklyn, I think I know what you're going to say. I figured it out after you took off like you did, and I get it. But I've been thinking about this all night, and I can't just let it go. Can I see you again?"

"You don't even know me."

He gives me that knee-buckling smile again, and I can't stop myself from smiling back.

"You said that already."

"What do you want?"

"Just to know that this won't be the last time I see you. I want to get to know you. I was hoping to get your number, maybe be friends."

Maybe I need a friend. Maybe, just maybe, it might be a good idea to have a man who looks like this in my corner if Cain shows up.

"I guess we can do that." I pull out my phone.

He grins, and we exchange numbers. God, his smile is intoxicating. He probably knows it too.

A few minutes later, I shoo him off, and he winks at me as he gets into his car.

Friends. Just friends.

* * *

CAIN

I haven't had the nerve to knock on her door. After Mom gave me the address she had for Brook, I headed straight over. I pulled this leased Ford into the parking lot and sat in it, staring at her front door. It's the only thing between me and her. So close, and yet I know the chasm between us is virtually uncrossable, thanks to my temper.

I don't know how she managed to pull herself

back up, but I thank God for it. Though the idea of me talking to God is a joke, even to Him, I'm sure. I'm the last one whose prayers He would hear, and I've never cared before, but somehow knowing she was in such a state has changed everything.

I don't know what I expected; I guess I never really thought about that part. Knowing she still had the rental when I left, I never sat down and thought about the fact that she didn't have a job back then because I would never let her work. She used to wait tables as a teenager, so maybe she went back to doing that. But you can't make much doing that, not enough to pay rent and bills and feed a family. So she ran, scared for her life. Ran with nowhere to go, scared I'd come back and finish the job I started that night.

I would've, if I hadn't been arrested.

I found the money she'd been saving. That's what caused it. Donovan had me convinced that she was squirreling it away to run off, even though there was only a few hundred in the account. When I asked her, she swore she'd opened it to save money for Carissa, so she could go to college and have a nice wedding someday. She said she knew if she told me, I'd have taken the money out and gambled it away, or wasted it on Jim Beam. I didn't believe her, Donovan's whispers in my ear making me see red, then black. After our fight, I took off, blew the money, and then came home ready to end it. She was leaving, I just knew it, and I wasn't about to let it happen.

Now I see she was probably telling me the truth. Brook would've been too afraid to lie to me back then. She'd begged me to leave her alone, pleaded with me to understand, but that son of a bitch Donovan wouldn't let me believe it.

I suck in a mouthful of smoke, almost choking on air when her front door opens. Fuck, I haven't seen her in over three years. My heart pounds out an uneven rhythm against my rib cage as I watch her lock the door. Her hair is longer, way down her back now. She has on a long-sleeve shirt with a light denim jacket slung over her arm and dark-wash jeans that hug an ass that's clearly been in the gym. Her body doesn't look the same, all tight and toned. Even her walk has changed. She has the stride of a woman now, not a girl, not a young thing beaten and berated but someone who's healing, and just might not take any shit.

Good for her.

She walks down the stairs, taking a hair tie out of her pocket and pulling her long dark locks into a loose, loopy bun before heading toward an old beaten-up Oldsmobile. It's dingy white and looks like it's seen better days.

I'll have to buy her a new car with the money I inherited. She'll be happy that I'm able to take care of her this time. I can prove I'm a man, that I've improved and learned from my mistakes, and she'll remember that she's always loved me. That I've always loved her. It's only ever been us—Brook and

Cain, high school sweethearts.

But then there's Donovan.

I pull in another drag, watching her start the car, then starting my own right behind it.

Damn, I love this woman. It makes my chest hurt and my head throb watching her. Has she been alone all this time? Did she wait for me? She must have; she wouldn't cheat on me. We're still married, after all. She never even tried to press charges on me, not once, even after everything I did. That must mean something.

For the first time, I don't think I want to hurt her anymore. I have to make up for what I did, for leaving her so afraid that she'd rather risk the streets than go home, or call me for help. I would've helped her; how could she have doubted it? Even after that night, she had to know I loved her no matter what.

I follow her from a couple of cars back, turn for turn. Eventually she pulls into the driveway of a huge house, and I hang back, parking on the street and slumping down in my seat as I wait to see where she's headed next.

***

BROOKLYN

I knock on Ashley and Shane's door, having arrived to pick up Carissa. Ashley opens the door with a smile, and I marvel at how beautiful she is, even with no makeup and her hair up in a ponytail.

"So, you got stuck in an elevator with Brandon, huh?" she asks as I walk past her. Carissa greets me with a warm hug and a smile from where she's playing on the floor with Ashley's son.

"News travels fast. Is there coffee?"

She nods, and I head to the kitchen to help myself.

"Tell me what happened," she orders as I sit down, mug in hand.

"So I take it you know him?"

"Yes. He's my sister's best friend's ex. She's Ava's mom."

"He seems nice." I shrug.

"He is nice. He's a sweetheart. Do you like him?"

I laugh, hiding my face as I sip from my coffee. "He seems nice," I repeat.

"Tell me the truth."

I meet her copper-colored, smiling eyes and blow out a deep breath. Then the whole story comes tumbling out of me, all the gory details.

By the end of it, my cup is empty. Ashley grins at me from ear to ear. "Oh my God, you like him."

"No I don't."

"Shut up, yes you do. Three hours in an elevator and you two are all open and sharing? Come on, he obviously likes you too."

I smile to myself. Maybe he does. But the news I haven't shared with her dissolves that bubbly feeling in my gut. Rising for more coffee, I toss the statement out as if it's nothing, not the crushing blow I've been fearing for three years.

"Cain is out of prison. The jail called to tell me yesterday, said someone made arrangements to have me notified, but they wouldn't tell me who."

Turning, I see her smile is gone. She knows everything, more than anyone else. Ashley listened one drunken evening as I poured out the whole thing: tales of beatings, being locked in a dark closet, cigarette burns, and rape. She cried with me when I told her about that last night, the one where I left. Being woken up in the middle of the night and dragged into the tub to have a gun shoved in my mouth. Staring into eyes that I used to love, only to be rescued at the last moment by the tiny voice of our daughter as she came down the hall from her bedroom looking for me.

"Will he try to find you?" Her smile disappears as she sets her cup down, her brow wrinkled in concern.

"Probably. Everything I've done for the last three years has been to prepare for this. Working out three hours a day, the gun, everything. But I refuse to run this time. I won't. Is that stupid?"

"Hell no, it's not stupid. One way or another, if he comes back, you have to face him. Just don't do it alone. Running won't help anything. What about Carissa? What will you tell her?"

I shrug. "I don't know. I've obsessed over telling her about strangers, but he's not a stranger. He's her father."

"Does she remember him?"

"Some, I think. She might know him if she saw him, maybe. What do I tell her? That her daddy is a psychopath? That he beat me and choked me and put me in the hospital? He would never get help. I don't know what to tell her. There are some things a kid just doesn't need to know."

"Maybe tell her the truth. I think she could handle it. Obviously not everything, of course. She must wonder where he went though. Doesn't she ask?"

I nod. "Yes, especially after we first left. I avoid it when I can, and when I can't, I tell her we'll talk about it later. I know I have to sometime, I just don't know how."

I glance into the living room through the door. My little girl. How do I burst that bubble, that perfect world she lives in where things like this just don't happen?

As if reading my mind, Ashley speaks again. "She'll find out someday. It's best if it comes from you, I think. When she's older, she'll appreciate it."

"Maybe. I just hate to be the one to ruin the happy little world she lives in."

"It's reality, Brooklyn. And I think she needs to know, for her own protection."

"I don't think he would hurt her. He never laid a hand on her. It was just me."

"You wanna bet on that?"

I shake my head. "I guess I'll find a way to talk to her." *Someday.*

My phone pings in my pocket. I pull it out and smile before I can stop myself when I see it's a text from Brandon.

Brandon: Morning.

Ashley peeks at my phone and smiles, the darkness of my past pushed aside for a moment. "See, he's texting you."

"But how can I start something with Brandon when Cain's out, lurking and prepared to do God knows what? Plus, I didn't even tell you that Brandon works for the same company Cain used to. I didn't tell him who I was married to, and I don't know if he'd know him or anything. I'd rather just leave it and pretend."

"You can't hide, just the same as you can't run. Live your life and screw Cain. Brandon is a big boy, and he can manage for himself."

"He said he wants to see me again."

She grins. "Do it. It'll be good for you. I've known him for a while, and I think it'd be great. Give him a shot."

I open the text and finally reply, knowing she's watching me.

Me: Hi there. I hit Send before I can think too much about it.

Brandon: Are you free for lunch today?

I bite my lip, staring at his text before responding. **I have my daughter today. I'm at Ashley's picking**

her up now.

Ashley's voice breaks into my thoughts as I wait for his reply. "He's a good guy, and his ex is sweet too. Please, just give him a chance."

"He wants to go to lunch, but I don't want to introduce her to him when I don't even know him. It's different if the kids are playing together or something." I take a deep breath. "Maybe this is a bad time for this, with Cain out of jail."

"You can't put your life on hold waiting for what might happen."

What will *happen.* I have no doubts about what Cain will do, but I choose to bite back the argument. No one who hasn't been through it can understand. There is sense in her words though; a harmless, healthy friendship with a man might be therapeutic for me.

"I'll keep her for a little longer," Ashley offers. "You're off for the next few days, so it's fine. Go to lunch with him, see how it goes."

I guess it can't really hurt, can it? It's just a lunch. Not a date or anything.

I take a deep breath.

Me: Okay.

Damn, I haven't been on a date since high school. No, not a date. This isn't a date, right? Just lunch with a male friend, that's all.

As I stand up, my guts fall into my shoes and I glance down at myself. Jeans, long-sleeve henley. My hair is loose, and I'm not wearing makeup.

"Come with me. I'll help you do your face. Your clothes are fine. It's just lunch, and it's last minute." Ashley rises, motioning for me to follow her.

Here goes nothing.

Hell, who am I kidding? It could be everything.

Chapter Seven
BROOKLYN

SITTING IN THE PARKING lOT OUTSIDE an Italian restaurant, I grip the steering wheel and try to calm my nerves. Checking the makeup job Ashley did on me, I think I look pretty good. I'm still wearing the same outfit, but I'm not so concerned with that since it was a spur-of-the-moment thing.

I shouldn't be doing this. I told myself a long time ago I didn't need a man and would be just fine without one, yet here I am.

With a deep breath, I exit my car and shoulder my purse. Inside, I give the hostess Brandon's name, and she leads me to a lovely little alcove of a table where he's already seated. My stomach flutters when he looks up from his phone, standing when he sees me.

All the embarrassment I felt last night comes back when I meet his eyes, knowing he knows more than I want him too.

"Hey there." He smiles.

I sit down, and he follows my lead. I take in his crisp black button-down shirt, tucked into charcoal slacks. He smells divine, even along the swirl of beautiful scents coming out of the kitchen. Not knowing what to say, I smile back and set my purse down.

"I'm glad you came."

I busy myself with the menu, glancing at his hands. I feel flushed when I remember how he held me. *How might those large hands feel on the rest of my body?*

I shake the thought away, doubting it will ever come to that.

"You didn't waste any time calling," I tease, deciding on the alfredo lasagna.

"No point in stalling."

"You're really almost overconfident, aren't you?"

He shrugs and his eyes twinkle, a look that speaks deeply to me. Something warming, calming. It makes him easy to talk to. Confident, cute, charming, and he knows it, yet somehow he doesn't come off as a self-absorbed, arrogant ass.

"Probably. Most of it's simply knowing what I want and not being afraid to go for it."

Our eyes meet, and I laugh lightly just as the waitress arrives and takes our orders.

"I suppose women find it charming? Sexy?" I sip my water.

He shrugs. "Who cares about them? What do you think?"

I study him for a moment. Is he sexy? Yes. Charming? Yes. Smart? He has that too. Passionate, warm, outgoing—he's quite a dangerous combination.

"I don't know yet. Finish telling me about your ex."

His eyebrows go up. "Go right for the throat much?"

I smile. "What's good for the goose, as they say."

"Well then, her name is Chloe. Like I said before, we had a physical thing that turned into more, but neither of us really knew what to do or how to talk about it, so I freaked and took a job in Washington. Six weeks later, she called me, and I was all happy when I saw her name on my phone, but then she told me she was pregnant."

The salads come, and he continues. "She was a virgin when she met me. The minute she told me about the baby, I realized what an idiot I was, so I came back. Problem was she hooked up with this guy she's been best friends with for years. I tried, but I couldn't compete with him. And that was that—I had to walk away."

"Did you love her?" I shove a forkful of salad in my mouth.

"I think I could have. I wanted to in the end. I told her I did, but now I don't know for sure."

"Have you ever…?"

"No, I don't think so. I've been with a lot of women, but that was as close to love as I ever got, and I messed it up. But I learned from it. I'm not scared of it anymore."

I almost ask him how many women, but I stop myself. That opens the door to sex, and I don't want to go there.

"Do you think you loved your ex? Really?" he asks.

I nod. "I did, which is why I didn't leave. I wasn't ready to give up on him, and he made me believe him for a while. Then it got so bad that I was just too scared, and I was avoiding being hurt, or worse."

The conversation becomes easier, the dark shadows that always bother me illuminated by the light this man puts out. By the time he forces dessert on me, I'm almost lighthearted.

It's cool out when we head to the parking lot. Thanksgiving has just passed, but today it's about sixty degrees. I breathe in the crisp, fall air, smiling down at my shoes as he lingers close, hands shoved into the pockets of his jeans. I want to hug him just to pick up the scent of his cologne on my clothes, hoping to smell him for a while longer and keep this feeling.

"Brooklyn, can I see you again?" His voice is soft, almost hopeful.

I swallow, unable to avoid looking up any longer. His eyes dance across my face, touch my lips, and then move back to my eyes. My heart flutters, stalls.

I think he wants to kiss me.

Damn, I *want* him to kiss me.

Nerves hit me like a linebacker on the football field as I realize I've never kissed another man besides Cain. What if I'm bad at it? It's not like I learned how to be good at things like kissing or sex with him. I'm an expert at lying there and faking an orgasm though.

"I think we can do that."

He smiles, then licks his lips. Reaching out, he takes my hand, his touch warming more than just my fingers. "I know you need to get back to your daughter now, but I want you to know that I had a good time."

"Me too."

I mean it. I really did.

He pulls me into a hug, tight against his hard chest, thick arms curling around me and his breath in my hair. When he pulls away, he locks on my eyes and bends down, kissing the inside of my wrist. "Bye, beautiful."

I bite my lip, nodding as he lets go and backs away with a wink before disappearing into his car.

Chapter Eight

CAIN

I SIT IN MY CAR, ENRAGED TO THE point of ripping the steering wheel out of the dash as I watch my boss put his mouth on my wife. Not really a kiss, but he's touching her. He wants her.

My wife.

My boss.

My scream is muffled by the interior of the truck, followed by Donovan's voice from the back seat as he puts his feet up on the headrest beside me. "You know she's doing it on purpose. Has to be. I bet the slut knows you're watching."

"Watch it." I shove his feet down, checking for marks on the leather. "That's *my* wife, and I'll handle her for this. Lay off and shut your mouth."

"You better. I didn't teach you to take shit off women."

But she's not just a woman—she's mine. I grip the

wheel, ignoring him as my dark-haired beauty gets into her car and backs out.

My first inclination? Punish her. Meet her at home and show her who's the man in her life. But my second thought gives me pause.

This is my fault.

I did this.

Why would she have waited for me? I'm a fucking monster.

But she's mine, and I can't sit here and watch him take her.

Yet somehow I don't want her hurt anymore.

"You're such a dumbass. What are you going to do, just puss out and let him take her because you feel guilty? Be a man, Cain. God, you're such a pussy to even think about this. It's her fault. If she hadn't pushed you, then she never would've gotten hurt."

I swallow his reasoning but choke on it. It's true. Brook always knew where my limits were, and yet she never failed to cross the line, knowing what would come down on her. She was all tears and apologies and begging afterward, but by then it was too late.

She's long gone from the parking lot, but I'm lost in an internal struggle—I don't want to hurt her, but it's her own damn fault.

I glance over my shoulder, finding him smoking in the back seat. Same as when I was a kid. I'd wake up in the middle of the night to find him smoking in my room, watching me. He said he'd come into my window and lie there waiting for me to wake up. It creeped me out at first, but I got past it. That's when we started sneaking out at night, getting into trouble. When I was fourteen, he taught me how to smoke; when I was fifteen, he introduced me to alcohol. Women fell in there somehow too, and Brook. I honestly think he was always jealous of how much I love her. It's sick, I know, but it is what it is.

"I'm just about sick and tired of your mouth. Keep your bullshit to yourself."

"Pfft," he huffs. "Yeah, what you gonna do? Shut the fuck up and deal with her. I'm not the one trying to fuck your wife. Worry about that."

He has a point.

I turn back, silence my only answer to his snide comment.

"Well, I guess it works out pretty well that you work for him, doesn't it?" He chuckles.

Time to let wifey know I'm home.

I start the car and speed out of the parking lot to chase her down, following her to the same large gray house as before. Must be her bosses' house, the one Mom mentioned. Club owners could afford a place like this.

I park far enough away to not be noticed, yet close enough to see her when she walks back out. This time she has an older version of my two-year-old daughter with her.

My Carissa. Pain so acute it's like a knife slashes

through me as I watch them smile, hug. She laughs as Brooklyn opens the car door for her. My baby girl is older now, a little blonde who still has my eyes; I can see them even from here.

The pain at seeing my family strangles me to the point that I can barely breathe.

Love doesn't just vanish, right? There must be something I can grab hold of to make her take me back. If I can get to it, remind her of how it was, this time I can be better. This time I can keep her.

Of course she loves you. She's waiting for you.

She remembers the way you touched her.

The memories flood back into my mind, blinding me.

***

I smile into the eyes of my sixteen-year-old Brooklyn, who's biting her lip and staring up at me shyly while we sit on my bed.

"You know I love you." I whisper the words against her throat, feeling her sigh in my jeans.

They aren't just words; I do love her. I ache for her. But I need this, to claim her for mine. Nothing will take her away from me. She can't be unmarked, not after this. Not if I get my way.

I slip my hand up her shirt, not for the first time. She lets me palm her breast, releasing another sigh as

I slide my hand into her bra, and the nipple tightens against my flesh. She pushes into my touch. Needing to feel more of her, I gently pull her T-shirt off, tossing it aside. She stares at me, and I can see her cheeks are flushed even in this dim light. Full breasts heave in deep, expectant breaths as I bow my head, touching my lips to the mounds of soft flesh. Reaching around and unhooking the barrier between them and me, I remove it swiftly, leaving my love half naked and panting as I suck on her breast, tasting it for the first time.

I go for the button on her pants, and she holds her breath. "No" doesn't pass her lips as I nibble her neck, opening her jeans and sliding my hand into her panties, finding her soft and damp and waiting just for me. She groans, never having been touched, never having known the pleasure I can give her. She arches her back, throwing her legs wide and offering her treasures to my fingers.

Before I know it, her hands are in my hair and I'm deep, kissing tear-salted lips from the pain of first claim on her body. Slow strokes eventually pull soft whimpers from her perfect mouth until her first orgasm rocks her beneath my body.

* * *

I come out of the flashback with aching loins, the phantom sensation of her body wrapped around me still lingering. Glancing down, I realize how close I came to coming all over myself and swear. Looking over my shoulder, I see he's gone. Must've gotten out of the car when I was lost in that flashback.

Good riddance.

I hate him almost as much as I hate myself. I'd give anything to see her look at me with those innocent, trusting eyes again. It won't happen though; I'm not foolish enough to hope for it. The most I can wish for is to have her agree to a life with me again. I'll take what I can get, and I'll do dark shit to get it.

Looking up, I see she's about to back out. I start my car and pull onto the road behind another car, following her to her apartment complex.

I sit for a while, wondering if I should go knock on the door. I want to see her, touch her, kiss her, and tell her I'm sorry, how I've waited to see her again and that I love her.

Unable to resist the knowledge that my family is only separated from me by an apartment door, I pocket my keys and rush to it. After knocking, I duck just out of view of the peephole, hoping she might still open the door.

It flies open, though I'm not faced with my wife but my child. She stands just inside the apartment, wide-eyed and curious.

"Hi, baby, remember me?" I crouch to her level.

Brooklyn comes around the corner, freezing when she sees me in her open doorway. "Carissa, why did you answer the door? I told you—" she starts with a tremble in her voice.

"Mama, it's Daddy! Daddy's back!"

She remembers me. I laugh with tears in my eyes, accepting the child who rushes into my arms for a hug.

"You remember!" I stand, lifting her off the floor. I don't wait to be asked in, knowing I won't be. Stepping inside, I shut the door behind me with a kick.

Brooklyn is pale, gaping at me as if I'm not real. My heart pounds in my chest, and I want to touch her, but she looks completely terrified.

Can't blame her for that.

"What are you doing here?" Her voice is strangled, hushed.

"Baby, we need to talk. I need to tell you some things. Please don't be scared." I step toward her, but she steps back.

I don't want to hurt you, not this time.

Carissa hugs me tighter, and I kiss her cheek. "Daddy, where did you go?"

I swallow thickly. Brooklyn didn't tell her. I want to thank her for that. It gives me hope to know she didn't bad-mouth me to our daughter.

"I had to go away for a bit, but I'm back now."

"Are you going to stay?"

I look at Brook, who's crying. "No, Carissa, he's not staying," she answers. "You have to go."

Setting Carissa down, I shake my head. "Not yet. I need to tell you—"

"Tell me what, that you're sorry? That you love me and promise it won't happen again? I've heard it before."

"Daddy, come look at my room," Carissa squeals.

Brook swears under her breath, watching helplessly as I'm led by the hand to a bedroom decorated with sparkles and unicorns, with toys everywhere. She's been well taken care of. I knew Brooklyn would be a good mother.

I pull away after receiving the grand tour. "Carissa, I need to talk to Mama, okay?" My little girl nods in agreement.

Sensing her behind me, I turn to find my wife watching from the doorway of our daughter's bedroom.

Together at last. Something like hope bubbles up inside me, despite the stones set in Brook's eyes as she watches me, her arms crossed over her chest. "Why did you come here?" she whispers harshly.

"Because this is my home, with you and her. We're a family."

She backs down the hall, keeping her eyes on me. "We aren't a family. We never were a family. What you did—"

"Nothing is unforgivable, is it? I mean, not really, right? I thought about you two every day and how I could make things right. Please don't write me off." My voice breaks by the end. There must be a way.

Nothing is impossible.

"Are you nuts? Don't you remember what you did?"

"I have flashbacks, so yes, I remember."

She blinks at me, as if the news surprises her, but then the cold returns to her chocolate eyes. "Oh, poor baby has flashbacks. Get the fuck out of here. I have PTSD and OCD thanks to you. I can't stand to see food tossed out because I damn near starved to death living on the streets. I have nightmares about you sticking that fucking gun in my face. I can't stop working out because I'm terrified that you might show up and beat me to death. Who cares about your flashbacks?"

I scramble, reaching into the darkness of my brain for something that might soften her edges. All the times she yelled at me about not helping her come to mind, and I push past her into the kitchen. "I can be different. Look, I'll help, and you won't have to do a thing. Have you had dinner?" I open the pantry, pulling out pasta and sauce. I can manage that easy enough.

"Cain, stop." Her voice is eerily calm.

Ignoring her, I open cabinets, looking for a pot.

"Cain, stop. This is over. I want a divorce."

Divorce. The word lands heavy, falling on me like a wet blanket. Looking up, I meet her eyes, seeing no fear there. I should be happy it's gone, but that word sparks something inside me, something old and dark.

"It's him, isn't it?"

She blinks. "Who?"

"I know about him. Brandon. It's him, isn't it? You and him, while I was away?" I step toward her and she backs up.

"No, Brandon is just my friend. We ran into each other recently, that's all."

The stone fades, fear flickering in my lovely bride's face instead. I don't want to hurt her, but I can't have this.

"Donovan told me. I know the truth."

"I don't care what Donovan said. This is over, and you need help."

She backs up as fast as I close in on her, and my heart plummets to my feet as I watch her façade of strength crumple and tears pool in her eyes. I grab her, and the color fades from her skin. It's when she puts her hand behind her back that I realize she's hiding something. I easily secure both her wrists in one of my hands, successfully cuffing her as I reach behind her, pulling her body to mine and breathing in her scent, relishing the contact despite the circumstances.

My hand closes on cold steel shoved into the back of her pants.

My lovely has a gun.

"You going to shoot me, baby?" I hiss in her ear. I feel her shaking when I pull her closer against my body. Even knowing she had a gun, the feeling of her against me is enough to calm me. "We going to start like this?"

"You started it."

I can't help but laugh. Feisty as ever. I love that smart mouth, but it's felt the back of my hand too many times for popping off.

"It's not funny." Her voice is thick with tears.

Reaching up, I turn her to face me, staring into those eyes I adore, eyes I've hurt and made cry.

"I know. It was a mistake. I was drunk, and it was…. Look, I'm sorry. I've had three years to think about everything, and I don't want to hurt you anymore. I love you."

"You used to say that too. All that. You'd swear and cry, and then a week later knock me out. I can't. *We* can't. This is poison. Whatever you think this is, it's never going to happen again. You almost killed me too many times."

She whispers the words so Carissa won't hear, but she might as well scream them at me. They hit me like barbs in the chest.

Never.

I haven't lost her forever. I won't believe it. There has to be a way.

"Brook, please. I'll get help. We can do it together. Can't you find some way—"

She glances down, and I realize I still have the gun in my hand. I decide to use the opportunity to get the truth out of her. "Are you cheating on me with him?"

"How can I cheat on you? We aren't together anymore."

Fearless, that's my girl. I've always both loved and hated that about her. I'm glad I didn't quite beat it out of her all those times.

"We'll always be us, you and me. Always. Nothing

can change that. No one can love you like I do."

She looks up for just a moment, then back down again. "I sure hope not. You're a monster. You need to go. Get out before Carissa sees you with that."

I shove the weapon into my waistband and back her into the wall, gripping her chin and forcing her eyes to mine. Tears spill onto my fingers. "Maybe I *was* a monster. I hate what I did to you. But I'm back, and I'm not going away. Do you understand that? If I see you with Brandon again, I…."

The threat dances in my brain, on my tongue, but then I hear my daughter's voice asking me what I'm doing.

I bend down and touch my lips to Brook's, tasting her soft, hot mouth that's limp and closed tight against mine, salty with tears. I move my kiss to her ear, breathing in her hair, its gentle tickle on my face as I hold her against me. "If I see you with him again, I'll destroy him," I whisper.

Looking back down into her eyes, I see understanding shining there next to the fear as she slinks away from me toward Carissa.

I clap my hands and smile. "Now, who's hungry?"

***

BROOKLYN

I can't believe it, yet somehow it's real. I stare at my daughter and Cain, my fork stuck in a plate of pasta that's growing cold. I can't bring myself to eat it, since I've been stifling the rising bile for an hour now.

The only thing that keeps me from grabbing her and running is knowing he has my gun.

"Are you going to eat?" he asks, snapping me out of my thoughts.

"No."

"I made it for you."

I meet his eyes, sad and hopeful at once. "No, you made it for you. You think making me dinner will make me forget. If you want to do something for me, then leave."

Carissa looks up, red sauce on her lips. "Can't he stay?" Her little eyes are wide.

"He has to go back to his own house, babe. Daddy doesn't live with us anymore."

She doesn't argue, instead pouting and looking down into her plate.

"Brook, I love you," he starts. "Please—"

"If you do, if you really love me, then please just go."

Our gazes lock across the small table. Pain floats in his blue eyes, and somewhere deep down it bothers me that I put it there, but the feeling is fleeting. This man, I loved him once. I gave him my all. I left my family behind for him, choosing him over them. My reward was losing them all, as well as myself in the end. All I can do is hope there's something sane, something human left inside him, and he'll leave.

He stands up, grabs my plate and his, and takes them to the kitchen where they clatter in the sink.

When he comes back to the dining room, Cain kneels by Carissa, touching her face sweetly. "Love, I have to go, but I'll be back, okay? We'll be a family again soon, I promise."

She throws her arms around him, making me sadder than I already am. I can't believe she remembered him so easily, as if he never left. I suppose a child just knows their father.

He eyes me over her shoulder, the blue bright yet somehow dark at the same time. It sends a chill down my spine.

"Brook, I'll go. I do love you, but I meant what I said." Planting both hands on the table, he stares deep into my eyes. "You're *my* wife. If I see you with him again, it won't be pretty. You are *mine*. Even if I'm not here. Got it?"

I watch him walk out the door with my gun in his belt.

Damn it, now he's armed.

"Mama?"

My child tosses about half a dozen questions at me once the door closes behind Cain. "Where was Daddy?" "Why did Daddy leave?" "Why are you mad?" "Why did you make him leave?"

I blow out a long breath and take her hand, turning on her favorite cartoon. It's time for a talk, but not now.

No questions now.

No tears.

I swallow the lump in my throat, then take a deep breath to get my hands to stop shaking. He's so much bigger than I am; no amount of working out will change that. Putting up a good fight is about all I can hope for, I'm afraid, if it comes to that.

Right now, I have to pack. I should get us out of here before he comes back.

Rapidly, I stuff all my suitcases and available bags with clothes, and with a cautious eye, we hop in the car and head to the only place I can think of.

Ashley's house.

An hour later, with my daughter tucked safely in bed, I sit in my friend's living room, holding a beer and staring at her wide-eyed, worried face as she takes in the story I just told her.

"Well, stay here as long as you have to. I can't believe—"

"I can. I knew it would only be a matter of time before he showed up. Honestly, he was way more cooperative than I thought he would be. If not for Carissa, I would've pulled that gun on him, but she loves him. She has no idea what he's done."

Tears burn my eyes. Will it ever stop? This pain caused by hating someone I loved so very much? The perpetual ache of betrayal, and hating myself for feeling bad for hurting his feelings after all he's done to me? Attempting to wash it all away with a sip of imported beer, I look at her. "He threatened Brandon. I don't know what to do about that. I hate to put anyone in danger. If he finds out I'm here, I'll have to leave. I don't want to worry about him coming here and making threats."

"Tell Brandon. Let him handle himself."

"I don't know. Wouldn't it just be easier to walk away from the whole thing?"

"What? Why? You can't let Cain run your life and run off a man who you could really be happy with. Are you going to let him steal your happiness like that?"

"So what do I do, let Cain hurt him?" Tears strangle me, choking my words. "I don't love Brandon. I don't—"

Ashley stands, crossing to me and sitting beside me on the couch. "Maybe not, but you haven't had time. You know he's a good man. Don't let Cain do this."

Right then, my phone rings, Brandon's name lighting up the screen. What timing.

I want to hear his voice, laced with that smile he always has on his face. Hear him say my name softly and ask to see me again. But Cain's threat bounces in my head, blocking out all the potential that was there for happiness. I can't be happy, not really. Not ever. Brandon doesn't need to be dragged into my dark world, be hurt by Cain's psychosis.

I flip the phone over and shove it away, looking up

to see Ashley shake her head at me.

"Don't do this. At least tell him what happened."

The phone stops ringing, and an ache starts in my stomach. I really like this man, and that's exactly why I can't do this with him.

Chapter Nine
BROOKLYN

THE NEXT WEEK, I HEAD TO THE GROCERY store to restock. I haven't talked to Brandon since that night; he's called a few times and texted, but I don't answer. He's too good for this mess, and I'm just better off on my own.

I push my half-empty shopping cart down an aisle and select my protein powder. A hand grips my shoulder as I place the container in the basket. Turning, I meet ice-blue eyes set in a face I know and hate. One that haunts my nightmares, awake and asleep.

"What are you doing here?" I pull away from him, trying to put some distance between us.

"You won't return my calls."

"Cain, I told you to leave us alone. You can't come back." My voice cracks as a woman with a toddler passes. He shoves the basket back, the one I've tried to put between us, basically pinning me between his body and the shelving.

"You're my wife. You can't just shut me out."

I have to get out of this. I scramble for a way to get away from him, knowing running isn't an option. "You tried to kill me how many times? What is wrong with you? You think you can just say you're sorry?" I whisper harshly.

He reaches out, hand falling on my forearm. His skin on mine is a feeling I absolutely detest now. "But I love you, and you love me. We can get help."

"I don't love you. I stopped loving you long before I left. Get away from me or I'll scream." I raise my voice to prove my point. "I have to pee."

He grips my arms tightly—too tightly. I wince, tears forming in my eyes, the pain from his strong hands stirring up memories of agonizing nights spent hiding tears and nursing wounds.

"Damn it, let me try, Brook." His voice breaks, his eyes watering.

Tears, really? I roll my eyes at the sight, something I never would've been brave enough to do before. I would've been awarded a slap for something like that, but he knows we're in public, so nothing happens.

"Please."

"Let me go or I'll pee on the floor. I'll scream. Look, I haven't talked to him, but that doesn't mean I'm letting this happen." I wave my hand between us. "You and I are done. We're poison, toxic. Deadly. Go away."

He blinks away the water in his eyes, then grabs my face in the iron grip of one hand and leans in. When he kisses me, I bite his lip—hard.

"Fuck, damn it!" He drags a hand across his mouth, smearing blood.

"Let me go!" I yell. Flattening my hands on his chest, I shove the wall of a man, but his feet are planted too firmly for it to throw him off balance. "Go. Away!"

A few people come around the corner. All stop and eye us. "Miss, you need help?" a man asks.

I look up at Cain—my husband, the father of my baby—and I hate him for this. I loved him once, so much. I lay in his arms and smiled at him, I let him love me so tenderly, not knowing he was a monster. I loved that man, love him still. It's this beast that I hate.

His eyes fill with pain and darken, but he backs off.

It's not until after he walks away that I realize I'm trembling and there are tears on my face. I push my cart through the crowd, head down, then abandon it as I rush for the door.

I go to the gym and run on the track, deciding that right now the crowd is better than the solitude of the road. It calms me, clears my head a bit, cleanses me of the fear and leaves only the anger.

By the time I get back to Ashley's house, I'm ready to go to work, but I find bags on the porch. It's my groceries, the ones I abandoned at the store. And there's a note.

Brook,

Baby, I'm so sorry. I don't know how to show you that I want to change, but I do. I won't hurt you again, I promise. I'll never hurt you. I just want my family back. Please take some time to think about this, and then maybe we can talk.

Cain

I step over the groceries, only to be greeted by Ashley. She pulls me into her arms, and I collapse into tears.

* * *

I guess I have a tendency to go on autopilot. When I'm stressed, I turn into this robot, struggling to hide my feelings and going about life as if nothing is wrong. In the few years I was married to Cain's fist, it was for survival. Now it's just a bad habit. At work I sit in my office, ordering supplies, talking to vendors, booking bands and DJs, but with no real focus on the tasks at all.

"Brooklyn."

When I look up, Brandon's standing in my doorway, handsome in jeans and a T-shirt under a leather jacket. His eyes are certain as he walks into my office and around my desk.

"What are you doing here?" I ask.

I watch, baffled, as he drops to his knees, pulling out my chair to face him. "Ashley and Shane told me everything. You don't have to hide from me."

"But—" I'm cut off with a kiss. Swift and sure, warm and soft, his hands on my face. I sigh as I fall into it. We're all mouths and tongues, his hand pushing into my hair, my thighs parting to allow him closer to my body.

Pulling back to stare into my eyes, he mutters, "I don't care. I really don't care. I'm not scared."

"You probably should be. He's dangerous."

"Don't run from me. I won't let him hurt you." His voice is thick and rough. "You're worth the risk."

When he kisses me again, it's as if whatever was between me and my desires crumbles to rubble. I come to life against his mouth, finding myself pulling him in, his heavy breathing doing something to me.

"Damn." The word is a whisper against my puffy lips. "Let me help. You don't have to do this alone."

Even with Cain, I was alone. It's as if I've been alone since I left home all those years ago, with the exception of the short period when he was different. Of course, there were obvious signs even then that I ignored, because I was young and stubborn.

"What if he followed you here? Or me? What if he hurts you? Brandon—"

"We'll figure it out."

"I'm sorry. I guess I should've said something instead of just disappearing."

He rises to his feet, taking a seat on the corner of my desk. "You should've, but it's handled now, so forget about it. Can I bring you dinner tonight?"

For the first time in days, I smile. "I guess so. I usually just nibble on snacks and eat when I get off."

He takes my hands and gently pulls me to my feet, tugging me forward to stand between his thighs. His soft eyes make my heart pound and my stomach do cartwheels; I want to look away, but I can't. He strokes the back of my hand with his thumb and whispers, "I'd love it if you'd let me take care of you."

Take care of me? Be with someone attentive and sweet who wants to spoil me a little? What's that like? "Maybe this once."

His smile is almost as warm as his laugh. I still tense when he hugs me, and even when I rest my head on his chest and my hand on his hard, warm thigh, I'm anxious, but if he notices, he doesn't say anything.

"*Tu boca es el cielo, amor,*" he murmurs.

I smile into his shirt, where he can't see me. "So, what time is dinner?"

Chapter Ten
BROOKLYN

HE BROUGHT ME DINNER, AND AFTER WE ate, he pulled me out to the floor to dance with me. Even after he leaves, my lips are still on fire from his kisses. I didn't even care that people were watching, or that my coworkers could see me. It was like I lost myself and melted into him with every touch. I've never known anything like this before.

Desire.

And the Spanish, it's like gasoline on the fire.

With Cain, it was all take. He took what he wanted and left me a used shell that had no real idea what sex was supposed to be like. I've faked more orgasms than I've ever had. I've laid there and taken it because my life depended on it, crying and hoping he wouldn't notice. I hated every kiss and every touch.

Now, as I lick my lips and savor the faint smell of Brandon on my hands, I realize I have no idea what

I'm doing. All he's done is kiss me, and yet I can't seem to control my reaction to him. I go mad with want and kiss him like a woman possessed, but at the same time I don't know what to do with my hands or my body because I'm clueless.

I've never learned to have sex, not properly, not the way you're supposed to, with a lover who draws you out and teases you into madness so you can't stop touching him. Something tells me Brandon is good in bed, and judging by the way I feel when I'm around him, I'll end up in that bed, disappointing him because I have no idea what I should be doing besides lying there and embarrassing myself.

I just don't think I can look him in the face as a twenty-six-year-old woman and tell him I don't know what the hell I'm doing. That would be simply mortifying.

At close to midnight, I get a text.

Brandon: Hey, I wanted to tell you good night and ask you something.

Me: Go ahead.

He replies in less than a minute.

Brandon: My office is having a Christmas party in two weeks, and I want to take you. It's semiformal. Please say yes.

Staring at my phone, I bite my lip. Fancy red dress, new shoes, lacey underthings, romance.

Me: Yes.

Brandon: Great!! It's on the 14th at 7.

Brandon: Hey, one more thing. If you need to, you can stay here. Call me anytime, and I mean ANYTIME. I'll have a warm place for you.

Me: I bet you would.

Brandon: I hope you call so I can show you, lol.

I grin, loving the flirting and innuendo, especially now that he can't see my reactions.

Me: Nighty night, Brandon.

Brandon: Night, beautiful.

I slip my phone into my back pocket, happy to have something to make me smile, knowing what might be out there waiting for me.

For the rest of the evening, I think of Brandon. In such a short time, he's become a welcome, warming distraction. At three in the morning, I get the bartender to walk me to my car, eyes all over the parking lot for signs of Cain. By now, he must've discovered where I work, but so far, he hasn't shown up.

It's chilly tonight, so I pull my jacket tighter and turn on my heater, which blows cold air because I'm too impatient to wait until the car warms up to turn it on.

When I get to Ashley's, I decide to clean up to clear my mind, then lay my things out for tomorrow's workout. I don't want to lie down—I know that's when the doubt will come—but I soon run out of chores to do and climb into bed anyway.

I suppose I fell asleep, because I'm awakened by the fact that drawing a breath has become a struggle.

Unable to focus my eyes in the darkness, I feel weight on my chest, hear the rustle of sheets, take in the jean-clad legs pressed to my sides all in the split second it takes me to reach over and turn on the flashlight on my phone.

I must be dreaming.

But that slow, drowsy thought is quickly replaced by gut-wrenching terror.

Looking up, its Cain's face I see. Sitting on my chest, he grabs my wrists and pins them above my head.

God, I can't breathe.

How did he get in here?

Shit, is Carissa okay?

Panic locks up my tongue, preventing the questions or even a scream from tumbling out. Tears spill from my eyes as I struggle, getting nowhere.

The scent of whiskey and cigarettes swallows me when he leans down, the depths of his blue eyes clouding with something dark and familiar. I shake my head as he closes in on me, dragging dry, chapped lips down my throat to the swell of my breasts in my camisole.

"Please, don't." The whimper in my voice makes me sound weak, and I hate myself for it. But my protest gives him pause.

Drawing back, he watches my face for a moment in silence. He shifts, then lowers his head to my ear. "You know what I'll do if I find out he's been inside you?"

he growls.

"I do." I know all too well. But I can't think about it right now. "Please don't hurt me." My voice trembles, and I hate that my terror shows. I'm supposed to be stronger than this. I fought to be strong. I've practiced shooting and worked out religiously, and still I find myself pinned under him, unable to get away.

I close my eyes tight, silently begging God to protect me from what I fear is coming as he shoves his tongue between my breasts with a laugh.

"I'm watching you, and I'm watching him. I'll make you sorry."

I have no doubt.

I look up into his eyes, strangely dark, even in this light. The almost sweetness I saw in them the other night at dinner is gone; now only the monster remains, running his nose over my throat before he takes my mouth in a rough kiss, biting my lip before he dismounts me.

I watch him linger at the door, then simply walk out as if it's nothing, closing it behind him.

God, what he could've done to me. For a moment, I wonder if my trembling legs will hold me, but I have to get up. I can't just lie here. What if he comes back?

I scramble out of bed to turn on the light. He's gone. With the position he had me in, I can't help but wonder why he just left. Breaking in just to threaten me?

After a moment, I decide not to bother with analyzing his reasoning. It's never made any sense, so there's no point in trying to understand it.

Using my phone as a flashlight, I head straight for where Carissa sleeps. Despite having a room of her own in the big house, she always ends up bunking with Ashley's son. I find them snuggled together in his twin bed, sleeping soundly.

I follow the same process that I do when I have my nightmares. Room by room, I search every nook of the house but find nothing. The doors are all locked, and everything is secure. Back in the day, he wasn't opposed to kicking in a door. I make sure to check for that too, but they're all intact. Perhaps he learned to pick locks, in prison or from Donovan. I wouldn't put it past him, knowing he'd want to be able to come and go into my life undetected. I turn each knob, each lock twice over, just to make sure. I check Carissa again on the way back, finding her where I left her. My OCD doesn't want to let me sit down; the urge to check again, to go outside and look around is almost more than I can take, but I take it anyway. I force myself to accept that he's gone, the house is locked, and he isn't here now.

I walk down the hall, pausing at Shane and Ashley's bedroom door, poised to knock. I need to tell them Cain was here, that he got in. But waking them up? Getting them all stirred up in the middle of the night? He's already gone; what would be the point? I drop my hand and decide to let them sleep. I'll tell them tomorrow.

Laying my head on my pillow, I know I won't find sleep, though I need to try for sanity's sake. Just then, my phone buzzes in my hand.

I furrow my brow. It's three in the morning, but sure enough his name is lighting up my screen.

Brandon.

Against my better judgment, I hit Answer, curiosity and the need to hear a familiar voice stronger than my need for sleep.

"I know what time it is. I've gone back and forth on calling for an hour now, but I had to check on you."

Alarm bells go off in my head.

"Why would you think something is wrong?" I struggle to hide the fact that I'm totally freaked.

"Honestly? I just had a bad feeling. I guess it's crazy, but I don't like that he's around and I'm not beside you to keep you safe."

He wants to be beside me. But Cain, shit. A sob bursts from my lips; I cover my mouth and stifle my cries. "Brandon, you're not crazy. He was just here."

The pause is long. I squeeze my eyes shut, forcing the tears out as I take deep breaths.

"Are you serious? What do you mean, he was there?" he finally asks. The softness in his voice is gone.

"Yes. I was afraid he was going to… but then he left. He threatened me, and you."

"Fucking bastard. Are you all right?"

No, I'm not even close to all right. "Yeah, I'm okay, I think. Just scared. I don't know how he got inside. I can't stay here, not after that."

"Come stay with me."

Standing, I walk to the window and peer out into the night. "What are you saying? We don't even—"

"I just know that I want to protect you, and I can't do that when you're not here with me. I'm not sure what I'm asking of you, but—"

"I can't just move in, and I can't leave Carissa alone with Ashley with all this happening."

"I know. Maybe I should talk to Shane and just come there. I… Brooklyn, you're different. I…."

His stammering and quiet tone dry my tears and almost make me smile. "You're not the kind of guy who seems to be shy about expressing what he wants," I toss out.

His chuckle is warming, chasing away the blackness. "It's early in this, what we are. You make me feel…."

"It's okay, I think I understand. We'll figure something out. Thanks for calling, Brandon, and thanks for worrying."

"Just stay by the phone, please? And I'm not leaving you alone, not one more night."

"I'm not alone."

"You know what I mean."

"Brandon, are you sure you want into this? I won't blame you for walking away. We only just met, and this is all so much, so fast." My voice shakes, and I hate it. Part of me wants him to go, be safe, but the bigger, more selfish side is screaming, "Don't let me go."

"I'm never going to do that, ever. Stay by the phone."

"I will."

We say our good-nights, and his voice rings in my head for a long time. He wants me to stay with him. It's certainly tempting, but it's also insane.

Instead of tossing and turning for hours, I take my insomnia downstairs and turn on the TV, curling under a blanket until the others wake.

Chapter Eleven

CAIN

I'M WET.

Headache.

The sick roil of a stomach that had too much whiskey and not enough food.

My mouth is screaming for water.

Memories flood back, and I groan as I sit up, taking inventory and trying to figure out where I am.

How did I get here?

I'm in the middle of an open field. A cow stands twenty feet from me, staring at me as it chews.

I obviously drank too much, blacked out. Why do I do this over and over?

In the distance is a tree line; off in the other direction is a dirt road. I'm in the middle of nowhere.

Donovan.

As if summoned by my thought to call him, I hear him say, "I'm right here."

I grit my teeth, checking my pockets. No wallet, no phone. "Son of a bitch," I mutter to the night. Not to mention its cold as hell out here. A cold front must've come in. The air around me feels about forty degrees, and I'm wet from the ground and have no jacket.

As I try to stand, lightning hits my brain. Like a knife stabbed into my skull, I'm blinded by a sudden flash and brought to my hands and knees.

I'm heading up the front stairs of the oversized house I saw Brooklyn pick Carissa up from that day. I walk right in, locks meaning nothing, opening door after door in silence until I see her, my bride. She's asleep, dark hair fanned out on the pillow, lovely leg sticking out from under the covers. I enter, close the door, and approach on quiet feet, not wanting her to wake at the wrong moment. I get into the bed, mounting her just before her eyes pop open—

My vision returns and the stabbing pain fades into a dull ache. The scent of cigarettes fills my nose and makes me crave one.

"What did you do to me?" I groan, sitting back.

"I took you to a bar, dipshit." He holds out the cigarette, and I take it, relieving my craving in one long drag. "You insisted on going to see her, so here we are."

"Why am I in the middle of a field?"

"You passed out on me. You started muttering something about how you couldn't go through with it and then blacked out."

I remember now. I had Brook pinned in the bed. My intentions were to take her back, claim her once again. But looking into that face, I couldn't do it. Seeing the utter terror there, where love belongs, I just didn't have it in me this time. I had her, she was mine, and I let her go. I walked away.

"Yeah, I just—"

"She has you by the balls. You had her, right?"

I nod, taking a deep drag and blowing out the offending smoke. "I did. But something's different now. Maybe the time away helped me. I don't want her hurt. I just want her back." My chest tightens, doubt crushing me like a vise. Something in me wants to be better, but this blackness surrounds and invades me, making me wonder if it's even possible. My soul is dark. She's too good for me, but I can't let her go.

He chuckles, standing up on long legs in leather jeans. "Cain, my boy, what's the problem? I don't understand your issue here. You want her, and you want Brandon out of the picture. You can't rape your own wife." He laughs, as if forcing myself on her is some great joke.

It's not like it would be the first time. I take another drag.

Standing, I consider his dead eyes, like a mirror of my dead soul. Not one damn good thing in either of us. Growing up, I idolized him, thinking he was taking care of me. He handled the bullies for me, granted wishes for me like a damn genie in a bottle. Now I see him for what he is—just a black hole. He's never going to help me. Pain, that's all he's capable of. I have to get him out of my life, but it would be like cutting off a limb.

I don't want her hurt anymore. Not by my hand or anyone else's. If not for him, maybe I could've really loved her the way she deserved. Maybe she would be in my bed right now, in my arms, pregnant with our second or third child.

"Leave her alone. I'll get her back some other way."

His laugh washes over me, making my stomach roil as he lightly slaps my cheek. "I've never hurt her, remember? Never laid a hand on her. Don't turn pussy on me now."

"Why are you here?" I shove his hand away.

He pushes long black hair off his face. "Because you invited me."

"Maybe it's time we went our separate ways, Donovan. I want my family back."

"Oh, come on, I'm helping. Don't turn around and start blaming me again. You're the one who made the choice, not me."

"I don't need you anymore."

He shoves out his bottom lip in a mock pout, then laughs again. "Come now, my pussy-whipped little man. You're nothing without me. I made you a man. I'm not going to turn and leave you like the rest of them did. I'm the one who cares, remember? The means to an end, right? Now run along and get cleaned up. You have to work today. Can't be late for

Brandon, can you? You need to get into his computer."

"Why?"

Donovan pulls a flash drive out of his pocket and shoves it into my hand. "Just do it."

"What is this?"

"The solution to your problem."

I look down at the device. "Where did you get this?"

My question is blown off into the wind, because when I look up, he's already walked away.

* * *

After walking for forty-five minutes, I figure out where I am and am able to make my way home to a hot shower. By then, it's time to get ready for work. I stare down at the mysterious flash drive, wanting to take the time to see what's on it. With Donovan, there's no telling. Instead, I pocket it once more, then grab my wallet and keys, making a stop for coffee and breakfast on the way.

I can fix computers in my sleep, even after three years in jail. Today, that's just what it feels like; my mind isn't present as I repair, connect, and bitch at people for opening suspicious emails that crashed their systems. I can't get this whole situation out of my head.

I don't want her hurt.

I don't want Brandon or Donovan near her.

I have no idea how to protect her.

I suppose I could just pick up and run, leave her far behind me. Somehow, I don't think Donovan would allow that. It's like he has a hard-on for hurting her, and I don't know why. And I'm even worse because I listen like some kid. I'm hooked on this relationship with him like a meth addict. It's killing me, and I know it, yet I stay.

I have to protect her. From myself, from him. From everything that is… us. Donovan is as much a part of me by now as my own father. At this point, I've known him longer than I did my dad.

Donovan isn't around when I get home after work, thankfully. Unable to resist any longer, I scarf down the burger I got on the way and sit down at my computer, inserting the mystery flash drive into my USB.

After a moment, I open the file, and it takes only a split second to realize Donovan's plan.

Images that make even a monster like me ill stare back at me, the innocent, sad faces of children in pornographic poses, one after another.

I close it out and remove the drive, sure to clear my computer afterward just in case, leaving the sickening thing on the desk.

Donovan wants me to plant child porn on Brandon's computer.

I can't imagine hating someone enough to do something like that. I should throw it away, burn it, stomp on it, anything, but I just sit here like a fool and stare at it. In the recent past, I'd never think twice about the plan. Donovan has my best interest in mind, or so I've been led to believe. Questioning things is new for me, and strange. I long for the simple peace of just doing what he says without thinking about it.

Now I have the questions and the doubt, and it comes with gut-wrenching guilt and pain. Being my own man fucking sucks. Being his lackey was simpler.

But there's no question—I need to dispose of this.

I can't do this to someone, despite what he says. I hate Brandon because he's trying to steal my family, but I know him and he isn't worth this. Not this kind of life-altering destruction.

Sure you can. Imagine how much more hurt she would be if you wait too long. Better hurry. Unless you want to be the guy who swoops in to comfort her. Play the big softie, win her over.

I shake my head. It's a damn good idea, almost foolproof. I could watch this guy burn, for no reason other than he fell in love with the same woman I did. Watch my wife cry over him, sickened, and then come to the rescue. Grand promises and tears, swears to get help for my issues.

Temping. Very tempting.

Standing, I pick up the flash drive and toss it in a drawer, then grab my keys and jump in my car, heading to the nearest dive bar I can remember.

When I walk inside, the bar is dark, and I know the bourbon will be strong. I order a double and knock it back, barely tasting it but enjoying the burn in my throat and chest.

"Got a light, handsome?" The smooth female voice pulls me out of my own head. I saw her when I walked in, and she noticed me. I knew somehow that she would end up here, by my side.

I swore I'd never do this again.

Cheat on my wife.

Yet here I am.

Blonde, young, shaped just right. She bites her lip, leaning over my table to take my lighter, showing me her ample assets crammed into a tight pink top in the process. I don't hide my stare; I just don't care if she doesn't like it. When I pull my eyes up, she's smirking at me, lighting a cigarette with my lighter and then wrapping her lips around it with her eyes on me the whole time.

"You seem familiar to me. Why is that?" she asks.

I shrug. "God only knows."

She smiles, taking a seat without being invited and tossing the lighter back on the table. "What's your name?"

"Cain. And you?"

"Jessica. I know I've seen you before. What are you drinking?"

The waitress comes back with a fake smile.

"Can we get two more of what he has?" Jessica asks.

The waitress looks at me for the answer.

"Jim Beam."

She vanishes with a nod.

"So, Jessica, what brings you to a dive like this?"

* * *

This stranger rolls off me in bed with a satisfied groan, falling to the pillow beside me. "Where have you been all my life?" she says with a giggle.

Not the first time I've had a woman in my bed since I married Brook, but somehow I feel a little worse about it than I used to. Of course, I never used to feel bad about it at all. I am what I am, and cheating isn't beyond me. I'm a monster; I'm a bad guy. I've accepted it, embraced it. No point in fighting my nature.

An unpleasant and unfamiliar feeling, this guilt. I tell myself that she refused me, so I'm free to do what I want. God knows she probably is with my boss. But still I look over at this woman in my bed and wish she were Brooklyn.

I can close my eyes and the hand she reaches over and touches me with is almost Brook's. Almost.

"You want another drink?" I ask, standing.

"Sure. Hurry back," she purrs, watching me walk to the kitchen with no effort to cover her body, which I appreciate openly with a smile.

As I pour the drinks, all I can think about is that I need to see her. I need to talk to Brook, need to see my daughter. It's the only way I can win her back. I need to speak with her, convince her that the time away changed something. Changed me, made me realize what I lost.

Lost. I swallow the word like a bitter pill. I didn't lose them, not really. Just a temporary separation, that's all. We'll be a family again. We must.

But what would I say? I've spent three years going over speeches in my head, each one sounding lamer and stupider than the last. I don't know what I would say; maybe looking into her face, seeing those eyes, smelling her perfume again would be enough to loosen my tongue and get the right words out. She is my wife, after all. I can tell her anything, even though I never did. I never shared with her, but that will change this time. Everything will change.

I sit on the edge of the bed, downing the drink, feeling the hands of a warm stranger drift up and down my back. The scent of this woman on my body, my hands—I need to shower, get it off me, but I'm tired, and she has her mouth on my neck, her tits pressed into my back.

I turn my head, thinking one more time won't hurt. I'll find Brook tomorrow.

Tomorrow.

***

Thankfully the blonde is gone when I wake up the following morning. Being Saturday, as soon as I'm cleaned up and dressed, I leave to find Brook. I don't know what I'm doing or what to say, but I have to find her.

That flash drive pops into my head. Standing in the middle of the living room, I'm faced with a choice.

Walking over to the drawer, I palm the device, turning it over. I can't be that guy, can I?

You've done worse. Get him out of the way. Do it. It would be damn easy, and no one would ever believe him. She'd be yours.

Mine. My Brook, smiling up at me, thanking me for saving her from him. In my arms.

At the end of my fist.

Cowering in the corner, begging me to stop.

Showering the blood off her thighs after I've forced her to love me.

I look down at the flash drive again. What if she's always been right? Just because Donovan tells me what to do, maybe it all really is on me. I'm the one who listens to him. I'm the one who causes all the pain.

What if all I've had to do is say no? Choose the right thing?

"You really think it's that simple?" He laughs at me. I turn, finding him sitting on the couch, arms stretched wide across the back, head cocked to the side with an amused grin on his face.

"What in the hell are you doing here?"

My head starts to ache. His laughter fills the room around me and makes the pain worse.

"I don't need an invite, do I? How was she last night?"

I shrug. "She was a warm way to empty my balls, that's all. I won't see her again. I'm going to find Brook today."

"You have the flash drive I gave you?"

I nod.

"Good, use it. I'll see you later."

I don't see him out, just turn my back and head to the kitchen as the door shuts. I'm glad he's gone. I hate it when he does that shit, just popping in like he lives here.

I take a sip of coffee, discover it's lukewarm, and spit it out. The flash drive on my mind, I hold it tight in my fist. So small, so unassuming. You wouldn't imagine it to be a thing that could ruin a life. A two-inch long piece of plastic. It would be easy for me to do it. It's not that I'm above such a thing, I'm really not. But even a monster like me has limits, things I just can't swallow.

Looking down, I snap the flash drive in half, then toss it down and grind it under my boot.

The pain in my head threatens to split me in two as I look down at the mess, the finality of saying no to one of Donovan's suggestions. I just kick it aside and walk out the door, determined.

For the first time in my life, I've ignored him.

I want her to know what happened, even if she won't believe me.

Bypassing her apartment, I head straight for the big house where I know she's staying. Pulling onto the street, I'm lucky enough to catch her jogging. She wears a bright neon yellow and black running jacket with matching leggings, earbuds in her ears.

Earbuds. I shake my head. With us on the loose, I thought she'd be smarter than that. I guess it's a lucky break for me.

I pull over and get out, catching up to her slow jog and grabbing her by the shoulder.

She spins and stumbles as soon as she meets my eyes, the color draining from her face.

"Babe, wait. I just need to talk to you, please."

She pulls out her earbuds, filling the air with what sounds like Guns N' Roses. "There's nothing you need to say that I want to hear."

"I'm sorry, for everything. I want to be better. It wasn't my fault, and I don't—"

Her laughter catches me off guard. Shaking her head, she looks into my eyes, and her hatred makes me want to weep.

"The Devil made you do it? Is that it? You're a grown man. Take responsibility for your actions for once in your life. Blaming your friend is just sick, Cain. *You* made all those decisions. It was *you* who chose to drink so much and hurt me, not anyone else. You have power over your own mind—only you. No one can change that. So no, I don't believe you."

I swallow her words. "But, Brook... I'll get rid of him.

I'll get some help. I've been thinking, and I don't need him anymore. I just need you."

"You've always blamed him, this guy who I've never even met. This guy who your mom said got you into so much trouble growing up, and you've done nothing but blame him all your life. No one can force you. You let it happen because you wanted it to. I hate you for what you did to me. I'll never take you back. I'll never love you like I did. I don't care what happens to your friendship with Donovan or what help you get. I'm done with this." She sniffles.

"Please don't cry."

She looks down at the ground, tears falling off her face and to the asphalt. "You were supposed to love me, not make me bleed. Go away."

"I know, and I'm sorry for what I became. I'll never hurt you again."

"You're damn right you won't." When she looks up again, her eyes are cold granite.

"Can I see Carissa?"

The urge to touch her is almost overwhelming. To hold her, catch her scent, and feel her skin and sweat once more. If only.

I see the answer in her eyes as she almost visibly ices over. "You used to do this. You begged and cried and promised me just like this. I wanted to believe you, so I'd let you back, and then I'd get knocked down again. No. You can't now. You'll use her to get to me. When we go to court, we'll see what the judge says."

The fact that I can't make her believe me is as painful as watching her turn and jog away from me.

I may never get her back, but I can protect her. I have to find a way to end this. When I'm about to turn back to my car, she stops walking,

Brooklyn is coming back. There's determination in her steps. I find out why when she reaches me and slaps the shit out of me.

"How dare you? Who the hell do you think you are? You must have no grasp of what you did to me, to her. We were homeless for months. *Homeless*, Cain. We lived on the streets! I was scared to sleep because I was worried I'd wake up with her gone. I starved half to death making sure she ate, because of you. Because you put a gun in my face. Because you locked me in a closet for two days, choked me until I passed out, busted my lips. You broke my wrist. And let's not forget the rape. You motherfucker, you held me down and raped me, over and over again. Sodomized me. Made me bleed. I couldn't even sit down. Now you march back here and pout and toss out an apology, and you think I'm going to forgive you? How's this: fuck you. Fuck your apology and your pain and your crazy-ass excuses. Go to hell."

"Brook—"

She slaps me again, even harder.

"Fuck!" I hold my stinging cheek, a bit dumbfounded. She moves to shove me, and I grab her wrists. "Watch it, Brook."

"Or what? You want me to be scared of you? I'm sick of being afraid."

"I don't want you to be afraid. I just want you to calm down."

She tries to pull away from me, and after a moment I let go, something behind her catching my eye.

Donovan gets out of a parked car only to lean on it with his eyes on me. I struggle not to look at him. *What the fuck is he doing here? How did he...?* Knowing how she hates him, how she might think we're ganging up on her, I turn my eyes back to her and hope she doesn't see him. Maybe he'll just leave.

"Are you just going to let her treat you like that? I know I taught you better," he calls out, chastising me like a sick version of my father.

I glare at him, then look back down at her.

"Cain, correct her. Don't let her push you around. Be a man." He starts pacing by the black Lexus. It's distracting, to say the least.

Be a man. He always says that to me.

I open my mouth to retort, then close it again, remembering Brook, who's watching me with a strange look on her face.

"What are you staring at? Are you even listening?" Her sweet yet pissed-off voice brings my gaze back to her face.

He calls my name, drawing my attention once more. That was a mistake.

When I meet his eyes, I know I'm losing control.

My blood starts to boil as my sense of reason slips.

"Yes, I'm listening. Don't fucking hit me, Brook." I hear my voice, the edge, the tone. My blood heats up as she takes a step back, the strength glowing in her face flickering like a flame in the wind.

"You're lucky I'm—"

I grab her by the shoulders, drawing a squeak out of her. Her face loses a bit of its color. "I'm lucky you're what? Fucking hitting me? Yelling at me out here in public? That you're pissed about shit from three years ago when I've done nothing but be nice to you since I got out? Just what makes me so lucky?"

"Excuse me? Get your hands off me, first of all. And I'm entitled to my fit, considering what you did. You think you can just come back into my life?"

"Yes, I do. I will." I grab her face with one hand and lower mine to it, unthinking. All I know is I'm furious. "I am. You're my wife. If you let him touch you—"

Her eyes fill with fire. "You'll what? Go to hell, and take your friend with you. Maybe I'm ready for a real man."

I squeeze her face for a moment in my blinding rage, then grab her by her hair with my other hand. She screams when I draw back my fist, and her voice snaps something deep inside my brain. In that split second, I redirect my fist and punch the window of the car behind her, spider-webbing it and sending fire into my knuckles and up my arm as blood drips from my hand.

I can't move my fingers, and she gapes at me with

wide eyes.

My head starts to clear as I hold her stunned gaze with my own, realizing this is the first time I've ever stopped myself, or Donovan, from hurting her. I didn't lose control.

Her eyes burn and flood with tears. "Let me go."

And I do. Holding my broken hand close to my body, I look up to see Donovan is gone and the police are coming up the road.

In that moment, my clarity dissolves into blindness as my head explodes in pain, dropping me to my knees on the concrete in a blood-curdling scream.

Chapter Twelve

BROOKLYN

CONFUSED AS HELL. THAT ABOUT SUMS IT up. I brace for a blow to the face, and when it doesn't come, I open my eyes to find him nursing a possibly broken hand with a stunned look that reflects everything I'm feeling. His blue eyes are as clear as I've ever seen them, but only for a moment. Then he screams and falls to his knees, while I step back to give him room for whatever this is.

He's on all fours on the ground when the police pull up. *Who called the police?* I'm unable to look away as he makes a groaning sort of growling noise and sits back up, opening his eyes.

My heart stutters at the change in his eyes, the same one I've seen so many times. That same sick grin twists his lips as he rises, cracking his neck with a couple of jerky turns. The cops aren't making any rush of getting out of their cars as Cain circles me. When he becomes the monster, it's almost a physical change, always has been.

God, what in the hell is wrong with him? How can a man end up like this?

"Ah, my beauty. My little dark-haired, feisty bitch." He laughs.

Now the cops get out slowly, adjusting gun belts and observing as they offer a "Hello, ma'am" to me.

"Are you all right?" the heavyset one says, watching Cain pace.

"Who called you?" I don't answer his question because I don't know if I *am* okay or not. It's probably been a while since I've been anything near okay.

He ignores the question. "What about you, sir? Are you okay? Your hand looks pretty torn up."

Cain stops walking, stares at me for too long, and then blinks. His black eyes are blue again. I furrow my brow, watching him run his good hand over his head.

"I'm fine," he states, though he doesn't seem entirely sure of himself.

"Your hand is probably broken," I offer.

The younger officer walks up to me. "Ma'am, can you tell me what's going on?"

I nod but don't answer. Something is clearly wrong with Cain. More so than usual.

"Leave her alone." He mumbles the words, gazing off in the distance, then turning back to me. "He just wants to check on her, that's all."

"Cain, who are you talking to?"

He sighs as if exasperated. "Don't play dumb with me. You've always been such a liar." His blue gaze darkens further, sending a deep chill down my spine.

The officer and I glance at one another. Hand on his belt, he approaches Cain. "You all right, son?"

I've never seen him do this before. Fear prickles my skin like tiny shards of glass.

"Cain...."

And so it goes. The officers placate him but get nowhere. Cain keeps dropping threats and acting weird until the ambulance arrives. They take care of his hand, and the officers tell me they're taking him to the hospital for mental evaluation, considering how he injured himself and was acting like he'd had some kind of mental break.

Did he finally just have too much? Couldn't handle it anymore and snapped?

I feel sick when they drive away what seems like hours later. Not knowing how to feel, I turn and head back to the house. Maybe a hot shower can help me.

Ashley is at the door with wide, worried eyes when I get there. "Are you okay? I couldn't leave the kids, but I was watching. Are they arresting him?"

"No, taking him for mental evaluation."

I feel a bit numb, saying the words out loud. Confusing feelings have taken over. I don't know why I feel sorry for him. I suppose it's because maybe he really is sick; maybe he can't help it. Maybe he has a tumor or something making him this way. I suppose there will always be that little shred of… something for him in my heart. My first love, father of my child.

Breaker of bones.

"Damn, you said he was crazy, but I didn't think you meant really crazy. Are you okay?" She puts an arm around me in a half hug.

"I'm just feeling a bit… heavy, I guess. Off. It was strange." *And sad.* "But I have to get ready for work. I'll be okay." I shuffle up the stairs, lost in thought over things I don't want to think about, yet can never quite escape.

***

I'm at work late into the evening when my phone rings. I answer eagerly when I see Brandon's name lighting up my screen, rushing off the floor away from the music so I can hear the rich depth of his voice.

"Why is it that I have to hear from Shane what happened to you today?" There's a snap in his voice that tells me he's upset, deflating my bubble.

"What?"

"Why didn't you tell me? Why did I have to hear things secondhand about my girlfriend's ex going apeshit today?"

I grin, stopping in the hallway. "Girlfriend?"

"Don't distract me. Tell me."

"I'm just not used to having someone in my life

like that. Even when I did, I was on my own. I guess I just don't know how to deal with it all. I didn't know you felt like that."

"Well, I do. I could've come right over. You don't have to be alone anymore, unless you just want to be."

"No, no I don't. Frankly I'm sick of it. Brandon, I'm sorry. I didn't think. I do like you." *More than like.* "But we've barely kissed, so I didn't realize."

"You call what we've done barely kissing? Hard to impress, are we?"

"You know what I mean." *Can he hear the smile in my voice?*

"You know we're closer than that, don't you? I mean, I know it's fast, but this…." He blows out a breath. "This is just… I mean, we're close. Aren't we?" he asks quietly.

"Yeah, we're closer than this. I guess I just don't know how to be in a real, normal, healthy relationship. I've never had one before. He's all I've ever known."

"I know. Maybe we can learn together."

"Okay."

"So, are you okay?"

"Yeah. It was all so strange."

I spill out the entire story after walking into my office for some privacy. He listens in silence as I share every awful detail about it.

"Hopefully he can get some help for whatever is bothering him." He pauses a beat. "Brooklyn?"

"Yeah?"

"What are you wearing?"

I laugh out loud, glad for the change in conversation, in tone. "Nothing sexy, I'm afraid. Can I call you later? I need to get back to work."

"Anytime. You're my girl."

My heart bursts inside me at his words. I close my eyes and bite my lip, wishing more than anything I was going home to him tonight.

* * *

I get home from work around 2:45 a.m.—the room I've been calling home since Cain's invasion, at least. I know I'll have to leave again because he's found me, twice now, and he won't be in the hospital long. I push that aside; if I don't, it'll keep me up all night.

When I get to my room, I see the door cracked and the light on. *Carissa must've been in here.* Having already checked on her, I know she's asleep in the other room, so I push the door open without thinking anything of it.

Brandon is asleep on my bed, fully clothed with his boots on. I grin, remembering how much it bothered him that he wasn't here to protect me.

He wants to protect me. He cares for me.

I can't stop smiling. Upon entering and closing the door, I pick up the scent of his Armani cologne and silently rejoice that my sheets will smell like him. His sun-kissed, muscled forearm rests over his eyes, his chest rising and falling in deep breaths.

This man. Ugh. He's amazing. And he wants to be mine. God, I could actually be happy. For the first time since… forever.

Before I go to take a shower, I toss my bag and shoes into the corner and decide to take off his boots. As carefully as I can, I pull one and then the other off, setting them quietly aside.

"You know, my pants are really bothering me too." He grins without moving to uncover his eyes.

"I thought you were asleep."

"I was."

"Sorry."

He uncovers his face and squints in the light for a moment, then locks his eyes on me with a slow smile. "Seriously, baby, the pants have to go."

I bite my lip, heat rushing to my face. The closeness of him in here with me is making me feel a little drunk, and I love it.

"I have to shower. I need to get the bar cooties off me."

"Well, hurry up, and come back naked."

I laugh at him while avoiding his penetrating hazel gaze. "I'll hurry."

"Please."

I grab something to wear and rush off for the quickest shower of my life, nicking my leg shaving at breakneck speed. Afterward, I stare at myself in the mirror and let down my hair, now damp at the ends. Am I ready for this? Him and me? A different man touching me for the first time? I've only ever known Cain. Could it really be so much different?

I take in a deep breath, unsure, then step into my purple camisole and panties, what I typically sleep in. My stomach is a fluttering, flip-flopping mess, and my core is aching despite my nerves. I haven't touched a man in so long, I'm probably going to disappoint him. But I think I'm ready for whatever happens—to rid my soul, my heart, of Cain once and for all and give it to someone else. Someone amazing.

Before I step out of the guest bathroom and into my room, I wonder if I'm being too bold dressing like this. I'm dressed for bed, so that's okay, I reason with myself, hand on the doorknob. Another deep breath before opening the bathroom door, and out I go.

I find Brandon with his back to me, shirt off. I can tell by the slack in his waistband that his pants are open, and I almost groan audibly. The muscle tone in his back is sinful, he has the shoulders of a football player, and his ass... just damn.

He turns, eyes on fire as they take me in, a wide smile splayed across full, tempting lips.

"Hey, baby," he purrs, "come here."

For a moment, my heart is pounding so hard I can't move, but after a second, as if drawn to him, my feet carry me to where he stands.

"You're holding your breath, love. Don't be nervous."

He touches my hair. "Nothing has to happen tonight."

"I didn't realize I was." I laugh, looking down.

Brandon cups my face, pulling my eyes back to his. He searches them for a moment, stroking my cheek with his thumb. His touch makes me feel secure. "What's wrong?"

"I'm… I don't know. I've never…. It's always just been so terrible for me," I choke out on a whisper, the hard confession knotting my tongue.

"Brooklyn, you've never just had amazing, hot, slow sex with a man who loves to watch you enjoy it, have you?"

My knees almost buckle. His words stroke me, pulling at something deep inside me that I've never known was there.

Pure want.

"No, never."

"I noticed you never touch me." He takes my hand and puts it on his bare chest. His skin is hot over hard muscle and a rapidly beating heart. He lowers his lips to mine but doesn't kiss me yet. Teasing, he hovers just enough to look into my eyes without touching my lips with his. I stroke his chest bravely, taking in the feel of him under my hands for the first time.

"What if you're disappointed?"

He runs his hand through my hair. "Never happen. And it's okay if you don't want to tonight. I'm fine with hearing no, so don't ever be afraid to tell me. I can just hold your sexy ass while you sleep." His smile makes me want to kiss him, but I'm scared. "You're the boss," he adds, running his hand through my hair again.

I really am tired of being afraid—afraid of sleep, of Cain, of making people angry, of my own desires. I stare up into his eyes, shining with desire, with emotion. Everything about him makes me feel safe. I swallow, pushing my fear aside, and kiss him, softly at first.

His reaction quashes my nerves, my fear and hesitation, and melts me. His hands on my face, his soft groan at the first touch of my tongue tells me I'm doing it right and gives me the strength to push my hands into his hair.

His hands drift down my back, then back up, fingertips grazing my arms as the kiss deepens. When I feel them on my ass, knowing the only thing between them and my skin is purple cotton panties, I smile against his lips. He gives me a playful squeeze, chuckling when I giggle involuntarily.

But then his voice goes serious. "Let's lie down."

My heart sputters and stops for a moment. Then he kisses me with a gentle ferocity and I forget everything but where his body is touching mine—and where else it might be touching soon.

In bed, I'm thrilled to the point of holding my breath when he hovers on all fours above me with a smoldering look on his face.

"You're so damn beautiful, Brooklyn. I can't get

you out of my head."

I don't respond. I can't. Words have stopped forming in my brain.

"*Dios mío, no puedo esperar para probarte,*" he mutters in Spanish, lowering his mouth to my throat, his hands to my hips. Flashes of Cain remind me of how I used to always just lie there and take whatever he dished out. Faking orgasms, hoping it would make him go easy on me, make him hurry up and finish. Even early on I never enjoyed it.

But now this man trails his mouth down my throat, caressing my shoulders and collarbone with his lips, his hands warming my skin. I don't want Cain in my head while Brandon is touching me, so I turn and meet his eyes. He doesn't lift his kiss from my skin, watching me with tender affection as I force my hands into his hair and down his back, wrapping a trembling leg around his hips.

I'm going to fall in love with this man, if I'm not getting there already.

He whispers more Spanish affections against my breast before lowering his body to the bed and slipping his large hand into the front of my panties, throwing me into exquisite blindness at that first gentle stroke of his fingers. He groans his approval when I arch off the bed, widening my legs and whimpering while he touches me, slowly and deliberately drawing me out.

Right before I come for the first time under the touch of a man in years, he stops. Confused, I look up, and he smiles at me, rapidly moving to his knees and relieving me of my panties, then diving between my thighs. I've never known this kind of… attention.

He growls, gripping my hips when I buck, groaning as I struggle between trapping his head between my thighs and tossing them as wide as they'll go, offering my body to him fully. His groans push me to the precipice, knowing he's loving every second of it.

With one delicious move on his part, I buck, grip the sheets in my fists, and arch off the bed in an orgasm that is sure to steal my soul it's so strong.

When it's done, I'm panting, aching with aftershocks, and crying. Embarrassed, I try to hide my face in my hands, but he sits on my hips and gently uncovers my face.

"Baby, look at me."

I shake my head.

He kisses my fingertips. "It's okay, baby. I get it. Don't be shy. Please, let me love you. I want to cleanse you of him. Be mine."

I gasp at his words. "Can you? Love me like this? I'm a mess." I start crying freely.

He smiles, touching his lips to mine. "Yes. God, yes."

Love. We're falling in love. It shoots between our locked gazes like lightning as he kisses away my tears, muttering in Spanish and making me giggle.

"Brandon." His name is a sigh as I watch him strip off his pants, take out a condom, and crawl back into bed with me.

It's slow and gentle, and deep in more ways than one. Our hearts lock, our souls tangling while he's inside me. I look up and brush a sweaty lock of hair off his face, gripping him between my thighs. He kisses my palm, not losing rhythm.

When we've finished, I'm sated, and I feel somehow clean of all the filth that is my past and what I used to know of love. He pulls me into his arms, and without a word, I fall into a peaceful sleep.

Chapter Thirteen

CAIN

THE NURSE SETS MY RELEASE PAPERS ON the table after asking me if I have any questions. Of course I do, but none she can answer. No one in this place can help me or answer my questions. I'm not even sure the Pope could help me at this point.

I don't even remember what landed me here. The last memory I have is of Brook slapping my face. Then I woke up here, clueless.

After seventy-two hours as a guest in this place, they were obligated to release me since I'm "not a danger to myself." Of course, they recommend I come back and see their doctor, and I promise to call and make an appointment, claiming stress as the cause of my "nervous breakdown."

As a kid, my mom brought me to a place like this, told them I was talking to myself, but they wouldn't let me in because I was only thirteen years old and seemed perfectly fine at the time. I never forgave her for that, always suspecting that her boyfriend at the time talked her into it to get me out of the house so he could fuck her without a kid in the way. I might not have understood had Donovan not explained things to me, but I'm almost certain that's what happened.

Once again I'm released with nothing more than my name and my wallet into the cool afternoon. It's getting close to Christmas; maybe I should do some shopping, get my wife and daughter something nice.

The cops towed my car, of course, so I have to call a cab. As I wait, I wonder where Donovan might be. Not that I miss him, but it's not like him to miss an opportunity to fuck with me.

Just as the cab pulls up, my phone rings. Mom.

"You want your money," I sigh.

"You've had plenty of time."

I tap the glass and ask the driver to take me to the bank for a cashier's check. I have to get this woman off my back. "Fine. Give me an hour and I'll be there."

* * *

Walking up the steps to my childhood home doesn't give me the warm fuzzies to say the least, especially when I see Donovan perched on the railing, tossing a cigarette out into the yard. "You aren't really going to pay her."

"How did you know I was—"

He waves me off, hopping off the rail and leaning on the wall by the door. "You ask too many questions. I have my ways, always have. You doubt me?"

"I just—"

"Well, don't think too much. It gets you into trouble. You aren't paying this bitch."

"I told her I would. I'd like to get her off my ass." I knock on the door.

"She doesn't deserve this money. You know she's been a shitty bitch of a mother to you since your dad left. Show her who's boss, and she won't ever ask you again."

The door flies open. In her robe at two in the afternoon, she steps aside to let us in. "Where is it?"

"Look, before I hand anything over, I have some shit to say to you." I plant my feet on the floor, crossing my arms. Donovan circles her, a dangerous look on his face.

"Just you watch it. I'm still your mother."

I laugh. "Yeah, you gave birth to me, but you're no mom. You let all those men do shit to me. You tried to commit me."

"You're a liar. Those men never touched you. You always lied. I don't know what I did to deserve such an ungrateful brat as you. Now you're an ex-con, and your wife and kid want nothing to do with you."

Donovan cracks his knuckles, smiling at me. "I can't let you just take this off her."

I rub a hand over my face, breathing deeply. "Let me handle this."

She holds out her hand. "Just give me the money and go."

"I want to know why you didn't help them. Is it because you didn't want to risk losing this money if I spent it on them?"

She scoffs, her pasty skin turning flush. "No, of course not. I was just doing what you said, keeping it safe."

"You're a liar."

I hold the check out but don't let her touch it. "You can't have it unless you tell me the truth."

"What? I am. I just…," she blusters, reaching for it. I put it back in my pocket with a sneer. "You told me to keep it safe."

I don't answer.

"Well, Brooklyn was always a liar. How was I to know she was really on the streets? She probably just wanted the money."

"She never knew. And why didn't you check on her? Because you didn't care. You wanted this money more than you wanted to see her safe, or your granddaughter. Your flesh and blood. What happened to you? You weren't always like this. Just because Dad left, you turned into… this?"

"Your dad was a monster. Just like you."

I'm chilled to my core. *Just like me.* "What do you mean?"

"He beat me, stole and embezzled and drank himself into a stupor, then left me when he hit it big. He made his millions and left. Of course, he blew most of it, but he made me like this. Just like you. You'll turn her into this too. She'll end up just like me."

The urge to knock her ass down is overwhelming, but just as I take the step, Donovan winks at me. I watch as he takes her head in his hands and, in one smooth jerk, breaks her neck. She crumples, eyes open, never knowing what hit her, never seeing him, never getting her money.

"Fuck, what did you do?" I scream, stumbling backward.

He steps over her. "What you needed to do a long time ago. She's where she belongs now, in Hell."

Shit, I have to get out of here. What if someone thinks I did this? How can I explain? People will think I'm a murderer. That I killed my mother.

Fuck.

"How could you do this to me?" I shout, heading for the door. I don't want to go back to prison. "How am I supposed to take care of my family and be with them if I'm in trouble for this, when I didn't even do it?"

Donavan sighs, as if I'm a frustrating child who just can't understand because it's grown-up business. "You worry too much. Let's get out of here."

"How? My car was impounded. I took a cab here."

Donovan throws me my mom's keys from the bowl by the door. "Take hers. Not like she'll be needing it anymore." He laughs as he kicks her limp body, and my stomach roils.

We climb into the car, and I floor it out of the driveway. I grip the wheel too tightly to stop the tremble in my hands, knuckles white. The sick twist, that crunch of breaking bones and the life disappearing as she fell to the ground play over and over again in my head. Even in prison, I never saw anyone die like that.

In a haze, I end up pulling into the mall. I don't know why I'm here. I sit in her car, just staring at the building until a security guard knocks on my window to ask me if I'm all right. I nod, getting out of the car without offering an explanation. I walk off in the direction of the mall, trying not to think about the look on Mom's face when she dropped to the floor, or the fact that she had no idea today was her last day to breathe.

It's two weeks until Christmas, and until now I haven't thought much about it. I shop and shop, buying all the crap that might light up my daughter's face, and maybe put a smile on Brook's. I walk out of a jewelry store with my stomach in a knot, hoping I didn't just blow several thousand bucks, that when she sees it, she might believe I've changed.

But have I? I was ready to knock my mom out. Would I have, had Donovan not stepped in?

I can hope I'm better, but I have my doubts. I didn't hit Brook, and I broke the flash drive, opting not to ruin the life of an innocent man. But until Donovan is gone, I'll never really know.

As I watch my gifts being wrapped, I wonder how long it'll be before someone finds Mom, and what in the hell I'll tell the cops when they come knocking on my door with their questions.

Upon leaving the mall, my car loaded with gifts, I sit at a red light, mind drifting. I realize I'm sitting beside an old brick Catholic church. Someone behind me honks because I'm now sitting at a green light. Unthinking, I make a sharp left and get honked at again, almost causing an accident to pull into the church's parking lot.

What am I doing? I'm probably going to drop dead as soon as my black soul crosses the threshold. Regardless, I get out of the car and find the church's door unlocked. Inside, it smells of candles and the polish they use on these old wooden pews. I don't cross myself. I pass the holy water without pause. I don't kneel at the foot of the cross, but I do take the time to stand, staring up at the image for a moment, with no clue why I'm here.

Christ hangs on the cross, bleeding for humanity. Everyone except me, I suppose.

"Can I help you, son?" a voice calls out. I turn, finding an older man behind me, short with kind eyes. Wearing a sweater and slacks, he holds a book in his arm. "Are you looking for something?"

"I don't know." I laugh at myself. Probably the truest thing I've ever said.

"Come with me and maybe we can figure it out.

What's your name?"

He motions for me to follow him, and I do.

"Cain. Cain James."

"Nice to meet you. I'm Father Donovan."

I choke on nothing but air and saliva. The priest stops, turning with true concern on his face. "Are you okay?"

"I think I made a mistake. Is that really your name?"

"Son, names don't matter. Come with me. Does my name frighten you?"

I open my mouth, then close it again. *Is he watching me? Does he know I'm here?* I've never been paranoid that I can remember, but this is freaking me out.

Hell, he's just a guy. Donovan is a lowlife, not some omnipresent creature who's looking over my shoulder. Don't I have to take the risk? Don't I want to get away from him and protect Brook? Even be with her again? I swallow. "Yeah, I guess it does."

Forcing my feet to follow is hard. My first instinct is to turn and run.

I need to get out of here. Something is wrong. How can his name be the same? Of all the names there are in the world, really?

He opens a door to a small, neat office. Offering me a seat, he closes the door and sits down behind a desk.

Donovan. The name echoes in my head. A dull throb starts behind my eyes, threatening to blow up into one of my blinding migraines. None of this is making sense.

"Now, tell me what's going on." He smiles,

leaning forward.

"Um… I don't know where to start. It's just so… strange." I glance around. Books and papers lie in piles, and there's a rosary on the desk. No hint of the other Donovan—yet.

"Just start at the beginning."

And I do. I tell him the whole damn fucked-up story. How when I was eleven, my dad left, and when I was twelve, Donovan showed up. He protected me from the men, from my mom, the bullies. Showed me how to stand up and "be a man." How I met Brooklyn when I was fifteen and she was thirteen. How we were friends, and then she finally agreed to go out with me, and then the turn. How we got pregnant in high school, were thrown out, moved to Dallas. The drinking, the women, the gambling, the blood, the burns, the locked doors, the screams. Tears, begging, promises to be better, and the gun. I tell him about prison, and he sits there calmly, listening to me as if we're chatting over tea in the English countryside and I'm telling him about my day.

"Mr. James, you want to get away from this man's negative influence, is that it?" he says without blinking when I've finally finished my sordid tale.

"Yes. I want him to go away. He's ruined my life." My voice breaks, and suddenly I can't hold it back one more second. Here in front of this stranger, I start to blubber like a baby, crying and sniffling until I feel his hand on my shoulder. I don't look up as I hear a muttered prayer, feel a damp cross made with his fingers on my forehead. He's praying for me, blessing me.

And it doesn't hurt, or burn, or anything like that. Just words spoken into the air. Just water on my forehead. I believe in demons, the Devil, and God. I know Christ is real and has abandoned me. I know it's too late for my soul.

"How can I make him leave?" I suck up my sobs, swallowing them until they're nothing more than a tremble in my throat.

"Well, we're all tormented, my son, but some more than others. Have you prayed? Perhaps just talked to Him, telling Him how you feel?"

I laugh at the notion. "No, God doesn't hear my prayers."

"Well, my son, Christ has a place for all. No one is so bad that he cannot be forgiven. You must ask for forgiveness for your sins, repent and go on. Then this Donovan will leave you. You're stronger simply because you have a choice. You decide what you are and what becomes of you. Ultimately, your choices are yours."

As the words start to sink in, I'm blinded by what feels like a knife in my head. White light flashes, my own screams bringing me to my knees amid the deafening sound of laughter. Faint, as if muffled, I hear the priest saying something, but I can't understand it. I feel his hand on my shoulder, hear a call for help.

In a moment, I'm back. The pain fades, and my vision returns. I see him on his knees, rosary clutched in his hand and a prayer on his lips. "My son, are you all right? I've called for help."

Getting to my feet, I dust off my jeans. "It's nothing. I'm okay now, thanks."

He calls to me as I walk out, but I ignore him. As I turn back into the main sanctuary, I stop once more before the cross. Christ is still hanging there, almost mocking me. His salvation is out of reach for me; there's no point in reaching for it. I don't even know why I bothered coming here. As if prayer is the answer for my fucked-up life.

A noise catches my attention. Someone has dropped some books off in the distance. Then a woman screams from the hall I just left. Curious, I turn back. A nun is standing in the door of the priest's office.

"What's wrong?" I call out to her.

She looks at me, wide-eyed and shaking her head.

I take the short walk, and upon reaching his office, one I left only moments ago, I see the good priest. Strangled by his rosary, neck broken, he dangles from the rafter beams of his office.

Holy shit.

What the fuck did he do now?

The nun's a sobbing mess beside me.

"Um… I'll go call for help," I offer.

She nods, thanking me as we both turn away from the sight.

I head out to the front of the church, but I don't call anyone. I just get the hell out of there as fast as I can.

Chapter Fourteen

BROOKLYN

IT OCCURS TO ME HOW MUCH I'VE CHANGED in a short time. I've skipped more workouts than I want to admit to, my confidence growing bigger than my fear, realizing I'm not defined by my terror. With Brandon by my side, I decided to move out of Shane and Ashley's house and back into my apartment. I really didn't want to put them in any more danger, and I figured it was time to get back to some part of my life again. None of this makes me who I am, and I refuse to let it, so living in fear just isn't an option for me anymore.

I'm me, no matter who's in my bed. No matter what I'm afraid of. And for the first time, I'm okay with who I am. Meaning I'm not having a panic attack over missing a run, or going into screaming mom mode when I see someone throwing out food. I have to get over things, and I am.

As I watch Brandon play tea party on the floor with both our girls, I can't help but wonder how much of that change is because of him. My daughter hands him a cup of imaginary tea, instructs him on the ins and outs of holding the cup properly, and sets a pretty hat on his head that doesn't fit, and he takes it all in stride.

On Monday when he comes by with his daughter after work, we put up the Christmas tree. Our daughters are having a blast as a Christmas movie plays, and Brandon is giving me eyes from across the room. The soft glances and smiles are warming, making me ache for him, wanting to reach for him, but still I hesitate. He stands across the room, and I can't make my feet move to where he is. Instead I turn, making my way to the Christmas cookies in the kitchen. In a moment, I feel his body heat and it makes me smile.

"Got a cookie for me?" he purrs in my ear, his lips sending a deep chill through my body.

"Maybe."

His "mmm" of approval against the back of my neck makes me sigh and close my eyes. He slips his hands around my waist and under my shirt, and I giggle at the sensation.

In this moment, with the squeals of the girls and the Christmas magic in the air, I know I love him. I can't believe it happened so fast.

My heart is cleansed of the blackness that was Cain James, washed clean by my love for Brandon Maradona.

I have no idea how to express it, or say it out loud, but I feel it. Though I'm scared of it. I know he's not *him*, but the last man I said "I love you" to almost cost me my life.

***

It's Saturday, the evening of Brandon's company Christmas party. I went out and bought a new red dress and shoes, had my nails and hair done—the works. Honestly, I feel overdressed and a bit extravagant, simply because I absolutely never spend money on myself. He offered me his card, but I turned it down, realizing I have some demons of my own to overcome.

The girls have been dropped off, his with her mom and mine with Ashley. I look at myself in the mirror on the back of the bathroom door, turning to examine my curves, the swell of my hips and ass, the amount of cleavage exposed, the way my hair falls in soft curls down my back. Silky fabric clings tastefully, with just the right amount of sexy. Butterflies are reenacting *Fight Club* in my stomach as I slip on my strappy new red shoes.

When I step out of the bathroom, I find my bedroom empty. The thong I have on is already annoying me, so I slip out of it.

"Are you trying to kill me?" he rasps from behind me.

I turn, panties still in my hand. "What?" He looks amazing in a charcoal suit and red shirt and tie. Absolutely stunning.

He looks down, then back up. "No panties?"

I flush. "Oh, I was just…. They were bothering me."

He's beside me in a second with a wild look in his eyes. His hands land on my hips, then slide down the swell of my ass, pulling me into him. "Wanna be late?"

Yes, yes I do. "You're going to mess up my hair." I look up into his eyes.

"You're damn right." He groans, pulling me closer. "Leave them. Let's go."

"You want me to go with no—"

His lips move up and down my neck. "Please. It'll be amazing torture for me."

I grin, pulling back before he kisses my mouth and messes up my lipstick. "I suppose it will be for me too."

His eyes flash and, stepping back, he offers his hand. "Let's go, so we can get back and I can get that dress on the floor."

I groan internally but smile and take his hand.

***

The company rented out a swanky banquet hall and provided expensive catering, a live band, and a full bar. The place is buzzing with people, some dancing while others are by the bar or filling up plates of food.

A huge and beautifully decorated Christmas tree sits in the middle of the room, and tastefully gorgeous decorations line the space.

"It's beautiful."

He squeezes my hand. "You want a drink?"

"Um…." I glance around, thinking.

His eyes are alight, as if walking into this event with me on his arm is his proudest moment. "Wine maybe? Champagne?"

"What are we celebrating?"

He grins. "No panties."

I laugh and nod, and he playfully drags me toward the bar. After I have a glass in my hand, I'm introduced to probably a dozen people, each time as his girlfriend. I get a shiver every time he says it.

He's proud of me.

I'm sure I'm glowing as he leads me to the dance floor and pulls me into his arms when a slow Nora Jones song comes on. His hands on my body, eyes fixed on mine, I melt into him.

He spins me and dips me and whispers things in Spanish in my ear that I don't understand, but he promises me are very dirty. I giggle and sigh happily when he nuzzles my neck.

"Brooklyn, I…"

Whatever it is he says, I don't hear, because Cain is sitting across the room staring at me over Brandon's shoulder.

My legs give out, but he catches me before I collapse.

"Hey, you okay?"

"He's here. How is he here?"

"Who is here?" Brandon spins. "Where?"

"There. Watching me, us. The redhead with the navy suit and white shirt with the collar open. My husband, the one I told you about. How is he here?"

"That's your husband? You have to be shitting me. You never said you were still married."

I tear my eyes off Cain for a moment to look up at Brandon. He's as pale as I feel right now. "What? Why? That's him. We are still legally married, but it's been three years."

"He's my IT guy. How could you not tell me that you were still married to him? I assumed you were divorced."

"I don't know, I just…." I touch my face with a shaking hand, my mind racing. "I can't believe this. You hired him back? How—"

He turns to me. "I had no idea who he was, obviously. He's just another employee. I never knew anything personal about him. I had no idea he was the guy you were talking about. If I'd known, I would've told him to go to hell."

Tears burn my eyes. *How can this be possible? Will every happy moment of my life be ruined?* "I can't believe you'd hire him back after he went to jail."

"It was just a DWI, and he's a great computer guy. That was all I knew. I swear I didn't know. You should've told me, Brook."

"We have to get out of here." I start for the door. "I know I should have, and I'm sorry I never clarified anything with you. It's just so damn hard to deal with." I turn, ready to leave.

"Wait, let's just get security to have him removed."

I stop and face him. "For what? He works here just like you do. You can stay if you want, but I'm leaving."

I walk off, not bothering to check to see if he's following me or not.

***

CAIN

The only reason I came to this party was to see if she might come as his date. I know who he is, but he doesn't know who I am, so for now I have the advantage.

After my third bourbon, I spot them on the dance floor. He's all over her, hands on her ass, her back, nuzzling her, whispering in her ear and making her smile.

They have the distinct look of a couple that's been fucking.

I crack my knuckles, images of his bleeding, broken body lying on the floor bouncing around in my head. I threatened to hurt him if he touched her, and here he is, groping her right in my face.

I slam back the drink, wishing it had been a double.

I don't want to make her cry anymore. I want her to look at me the way she looks at him.

But I really, *really* want to make him bleed for touching my wife.

When she sees me, my chest tightens. She turns to him, they seem to argue, and then she storms off.

I'm on my feet in a second to intercept her before she gets outside. When I'm a foot away, she shakes her head at me, tears in her eyes. "Leave me alone." It's more of a growled threat than a request.

"I need to talk to you." I reach for her arm with my free hand, the one not in a cast, but she pulls out of reach.

"No. Can't I have one night? Do you have to ruin every moment of my life?"

Brandon walks up, trying to get between us. "Hey, man, take no for an answer."

My blood starts to boil in my veins, and I step up so I'm toe-to-toe with him. "This is between me and my wife. Back off." Spit flies from my lips and lands on his suit.

"She doesn't want to talk to you."

"She doesn't know what she wants. She hasn't heard me out yet." I pull the small box out of my pocket. "I got you this, baby."

I never got her the engagement ring she wanted when we were young. I sank lower and lower into the red and couldn't have afforded it even if I'd wanted to.

I shove Brandon out of the way and grab her hand, then drop to my knees there on the shiny floor, a hundred eyes on us.

My bride's eyes go wide, and she looks up at him as if to ask what to do. I take out the ring, diamond and platinum, and put it on her bare finger. "Brook, I never got to give you what you needed. I was messed up, and I hurt you. I just want another shot. Give me a chance to try again, and if I mess up, I promise I'll leave and you won't ever see me again. I love you. Please don't do this with him."

Her brown eyes stunned, she looks down at her hand, then at me, then up at him. For a second, I think maybe she's heard me, finally heard me, but then her face wrinkles in painful sobs and she takes the ring off, tossing it at me. "No."

The word is simple, clear, and she turns and runs from the room, leaving me on the floor with a ring in my hand next to Brandon.

I can't stop myself from imagining the worst. This man touching my wife, his hands and mouth on her skin. Violating what's mine.

Jumping to my feet, I grab him by the shirt. "Keep your dick away from my wife."

"Look, Cain, can't you see she's finished with you? Be an adult, a man, and just walk away and find someone else. Maybe it's just not meant to be."

"Not meant to be? I'll tell you something. We were

each other's first. High school sweethearts. She chose me. She ran off with me, had my baby. You're nothing to her. I was her whole world, just like she's mine. I know she won't walk away from that—she can't. So you need to just get out of my way so I can put this back together."

I put my hands on his chest, a solid mass of muscle, and shove him as hard as I can. He moves a bit but comes right back with more determination on his face.

"That might've been true, until you hurt her. Until you choked her, burned her, locked her up. She lost that love with every broken bone and bruise, Cain. You fucked up. Accept it and go on. She doesn't love you."

Glancing around at the crowd around us, I grit my teeth and slam my fist into his face, all my weight behind it. His teeth cut the knuckle on my good hand. I know I can't fight him with my other hand being broken, but at least I could get in one good punch. The fucker deserves it for touching my wife.

Turning his head, he spits, then wipes blood off his mouth. "You're fired, you know that, right? Go home, Cain." Spinning on his expensive shoes, he walks out the door.

Turning, I see all eyes on me. Some people are taking videos, and at least one person is on the phone with the police.

Police. I have to get out of here. I can't end up in jail for the murders Donovan committed.

As fast as I can, I head for the door, away from all this.

Chapter Fifteen

BROOKLYN

I'M IN THE KITCHEN IN OLD SWEAT pants and a T-shirt, my hair pulled up in a sloppy bun, when I hear Brandon at the door. I left Carissa at Ashley's for the evening. I swallow the water in the cup in my hand and take in a deep breath, moving to let him in. Opening the door without looking at him, I turn back to the kitchen, walking away. I don't look at him, just refill my glass of water as if it takes my full concentration. I hear his heavy steps come up behind me, only glancing his way when he puts a hand on my arm.

His nose is swollen, and he looks to have the start of a black eye.

"He hit you?" I ask with a sigh, though I'm not surprised at all.

"Yeah, no big deal. I've had a few busted lips in my life, mostly thanks to my brother. Are you okay?" His eyes are filled with concern, as is his voice.

Am I? I look up in silence, wondering. Not long ago, I might not have been, but now I feel as if I could be. Is that because of Brandon? Or is it me?

I swallow, then take a drink of the cool water. "I just want peace, and I'll never get it. I don't know why you keep coming back to me. It's too much."

"I can handle anything. I'm stubborn. No one tells me what I can't have."

I almost smile but hide it by looking away as I set the cup down. "I picked up on that. But, Brandon, I'm not a safe place to be."

"Why not divorce him?"

I look up, not knowing how to properly explain it to him. "I guess I was scared of what it would push him to do. I kept remembering all the things he told me he would do if I left him. I know we aren't together, but I know him. He's assuming there's hope because we *are* still married, and that would be like putting a nail in my own coffin. I guess I've just been scared. I'm a dangerous person to be with, Brandon."

With a gentle hand, he lifts my chin, forcing my eyes to his. "I'll be the judge of that."

"But why?" The next words tumble out of my mouth, shocking me more than him. "I'm not even good in bed. Why would you risk so much for me?"

He blinks, cocking his head to one side. "What?"

"I know I have to be a disappointment to you in bed. I can imagine the women you must be used to, and I'm just not… proficient."

He shakes his head. "Baby, you really have no idea?"

"Of what? I just…. You're so amazing, and I'm not, um, experienced."

"Brooklyn, love, you're like a feral she-wolf in bed. You come alive when I touch you. Can't you tell that I lose my mind?"

"Me? Really? I am?"

He smiles at my surprise, bending to touch his lips to mine. "Hell yes. God, the way you taste, how you wrap around me, it makes me crazy. You just have no confidence. I can't keep my damn tongue off you because making you come makes me want to fuck you."

I take in a sharp breath, holding it because when he looks at me like this, I can't freaking breathe. My heart falls into my shoes and clouds roll into my brain, fogging everything but him and the smoldering look he's giving me.

"Damn, Brandon."

"It's the truth. Come upstairs with me."

***

Later that night, both sweaty and sated, I lie curled in his arms. Head on his chest, I listen to his heart, the beat slow and thick, and wonder if he's asleep until he speaks.

"Brook?"

"Hmm."

"I love you."

Everything stops. My stomach does a cartwheel, my heart explodes, and I can't breathe again.

He loves me.

I pull back to look at his face and find he's watching me with soft eyes.

"Don't say anything. I just wanted to tell you. I don't need you to say it back. You're going through too much." He plants a kiss on my forehead, and I silently snuggle closer. I do think I love him, but he's right. I'm just not ready to say it yet, and I'm grateful for the lack of pressure. I know one thing for sure—I need to claim my life once again.

Brandon makes me forget that I'm mad. Forget that Cain is out there, watching, waiting, preparing to do God knows what. Forget that I'm damaged goods, that I don't know how to love anyone anymore until I'm with him and I'm just right in the middle of it.

Then he goes and does something like actually tell me that he loves me. Tangled with him and then hearing those words makes me wonder, what if? Maybe I can be something more than what I was, which was nothing but a punching bag.

***

On Monday, I drop Carissa off at school and go for my morning run as usual, then return home to change into fresh workout clothes. I'm headed out the door to the gym when I spy Cain sitting on the bottom steps outside my apartment.

This time I don't even feel the sick terror I'm used to. I'm just numb and frankly exhausted from this fight.

"How long have you been here?" I ask from the top of the stairs. "I didn't see you when I came in. Were you watching me?"

He doesn't turn as he says, "Since you left to go run. I was sitting in the car, hoping maybe if I waited patiently, you might talk to me."

Shit. I blow out a breath, clutching my pepper spray in my pocket as I start down the stairs.

"You loved me once. Can't we just talk?"

"As long as that's all it is." I sit behind him so he has to turn and look up at me. His eyes are bright blue and threaded with pain, regret—everything I've seen in them a dozen times before. He was always sorry for what he did, but never sorry enough to stop. His pain doesn't do anything to me, not anymore. "What do you want?"

"I don't know why I'm here. I feel like there are a million things I need to say, but I don't know how to say them to you. You did love me once, didn't you?"

"You know I did. I left my family behind for you. I don't think I can ever go back to them, not after they kicked me out of the house while I was pregnant. I'm not sure what you want from me, but you know I can't take you back. Something in you must realize that."

He nods, which throws me off. He's never agreed before. Not once. "I know. Part of me hopes you won't ever, the part that loves you the most."

"I don't understand."

"I know you aren't safe with me, Brook. Even if I change and get help. Even if I really mean it and I never touch you again, you aren't safe because I can't get rid of him. I don't want you hurt, and being around me is the worst place for you. But I love you, and I always will."

Him. I'm sure he means Donovan. I've never asked him much about his friend, but I always hated that he blamed what he did on this other man. Hearing him actually take the blame for once makes me want to ask the questions I never did before. Makes me want to understand what's happening in his head.

"You mean Donovan, right?"

He nods.

"Why don't you just tell him to go away?"

"I have, but he won't."

"Why does he want you to hurt me? He's never even met me."

"I expect it's control. He says I should demand respect, and anything less should be punished."

"Control? Don't you realize that losing your temper is the furthest thing from control?"

He shrugs. "It's all I know. I need help, Brook. And I'm willing to get help, but I know Donovan won't let me. He says head doctors are for pussies. He makes me...." He sighs instead of finishing the sentence. "I know I need to get him out of my life, but I don't see that happening. I tell him to leave, but he comes back anyway."

He blows out a breath, then stares off into the distance. "He showed up when I was twelve, after my dad left and my mom's boyfriends started showing up. He was all I had back then. He helped me when I was alone and dealing with the shit those men did, that my mom let them do, plus the kids at school. He did more for me than my own father ever did, but now I see what he really is, and I want him gone. I'm afraid it might be too late though. He won't go, and he's getting worse. That's why I'm here. You stay away from me, okay? He's going to punish me for coming here, but I'll deal with it. Here." He takes the ring out of his pocket and offers it to me. "Save this for Carissa. Give it to her when she's grown, from me. Tell her I loved her even though I could never be around. And I have Christmas gifts for her in the car. Can you give them to her?"

I've never seen him like this, thinking of someone besides himself. There are hints of the boy I used to know in his features, the things I saw in between the hate and rage and anger that made me stay, made me love him despite the pain. I take the ring, wishing things had been different, that we could've been a family. But it's too late for that now; nothing can change what is.

"Yes, of course. I'll tell her they're from you. I think you need help, Cain. Go see someone, maybe a doctor. And maybe the police can make Donovan go away for good. There are laws against things like what he's doing to you."

He laughs before standing up, fishing his keys out of his pocket. "I wish. If I thought that was true, I'd probably go. Let me get the bags. I'll be right back."

He jogs to the parking lot, coming back with several large bags full of packages wrapped in Christmas paper. "Brook, is he a good man?"

I look down, realizing then that I have nothing to hide, no reason not to tell him. He made his bed, as they say. "Yes, he's the best of men."

"Will he take care of you?"

"I think so, but I suppose time will tell. I don't need him to take care of me. I learned how to take care of myself."

He smiles. "I see that. I know my apologies mean nothing, but I'm sorry. And until I get Donovan off my back, I can't promise more shit won't go down. I just needed you to know."

I don't understand, but I agree anyway, watching him walk to his car with more questions than I had before.

***

CAIN

I knew I'd regret it, but I had to do something while I was thinking clearly. On my knees, the pain in my head is blinding here in the darkness of my little one-bedroom apartment. His footsteps are heavy as he paces, circling me, the smell of cigarettes trailing behind him.

"You just gave her to him? Is that what we worked for? Is that why you beat her and claimed her, just to give her away like some whore?"

He crouches in front of me, but I can't look because it hurts too much. My head feels like it's going to split open. "I just want her safe." I spit the words out between gasps and flashes of light and dark in my field of vision. The migraine makes me nauseous, bile rising into my throat. "You have no say in what I do with my life. Leave me alone. Leave *us* alone. Just go away."

"Safe? Safe is with you, keeping her in line. You want her treated like a whore? You want her spreading her legs for him? Sucking his cock instead of yours? Moaning his name? Imagine it, can you? Legs wide, begging him for it. Did she ever beg you, Cain? Ever crawl to you and ask for it?"

"No, Donovan, stop." I gag, my mouth full of saliva, sweat breaking out on my skin. *He hasn't laid a hand on me, so why does it hurt? Why am I about to puke?*

"You know why she didn't? Look at me!"

I look up, only to succeed in vomiting all over myself. "Why does it hurt so much?"

He laughs. The sound of it dims my vision, sending me onto my back before I can take off my shirt or wipe my face. He bends over me, and the room spins and tips, my headache dulling as reality bends, his face morphing into something dark, evil... monstrous. I can't do anything but lie here; even my scream is silent to my own ears.

What the fuck is happening to me?

"She never came to you because you're pathetic. You're not a man. Look at you. You have no more fight in you than a child crying for his mommy. Oh, and you cried when you thought I wasn't looking, didn't you? For the woman who let her boyfriends molest you, turning a blind eye because he had money, or looks, or fucked her just right. You're used and sad and nothing. How could she ever want you? You sat there and gave her to him. You're just like those men, like your mom. Giving her away when you're supposed to protect her. No one can keep her safe but you and me, remember?"

Safe. Keep her safe. That is what I want, isn't it? How can I ever be sure if I'm not there with her?

"Keeping her inside was for her own protection," I mutter.

"Now you're thinking clearly. And you had to punish her, remember? You warned her, and she broke the rules. You're not a man if you can't command respect in your own house."

Respect. She never did respect me.

I sit up, pulling my shirt off and using it to wipe my face. The pain in my head stops, my stomach no longer hurting as he stares deep into my eyes. "You're right," I tell him. "She's been away from me for too long. She doesn't remember."

"Brandon has to go. Make him dump her, and she'll come running back. You know how to make her beg, don't you?"

I nod. "I do."

"You want her panting after your dick, not his, right?"

"Damn right."

Donovan slaps me on the back, helping me get to my feet with a tug of his hand. "Shower and go take care of it."

Trust Donovan to make me see sense. I don't know what I was thinking.

Maybe it was all just the migraine. The vision, the sickness, the confusion. Now the pain is gone.

I head to the bathroom and turn on the shower, the hot water washing the filth from my body, the fog from my brain.

It's all clear now.

Everything.

Chapter Sixteen

CAIN

IT WASN'T HARD TO GET IN, EVEN THOUGH he fired me. When he walks into his office and sees me with my feet on his desk, pretty boy stops in his tracks, then shuts his door.

"What the ever-loving fuck are you doing in here? I fired you. HR has your papers." He looks as if he doesn't know if he should take a step toward me or not. After a minute, he walks around and knocks my feet off the desk.

"We need to have a chat," I say matter-of-factly.

"God, you're thickheaded. Get out or I'm calling security."

"Aw, you scared? Can't handle me yourself?" I mock, sticking my lip out in a pout.

"What do you want?"

I stand up so we're nose-to-nose. He reeks of cologne. "I want you to break it off with her. Step out of the picture."

"Oh, that's funny. Thanks, I needed that." He chuckles, crossing his arms. "No, really, why are you here?"

"You're going to bow out, and I'm coming back home. You're going to break it off with her."

"No."

"Look, I know you think I'm not really dangerous, that maybe I only beat up women. I'd hate to prove otherwise, so I'll just say this. Leave her, because if you take someone from me, I'm damn sure going to take someone from you. And it's going to hurt, and they won't be coming back."

"You're—" He wrinkles his brow.

"I'll trade you. Fair and simple. Someone I love for someone you love. And when they… well, I'll make sure they know it's because you chose this. Mark my words. I'm sure Brook has told you horror stories about me by now. That's just the tip of the iceberg. She has no idea what I've done, or what I'm capable of. So go ahead and risk it, because in the end, I'll still win. I might have to shed some blood along the way, more than intended, but whatever."

He goes a shade lighter, and his eyes widen, then darken a bit with hidden rage. I can smell the fear on him. I pat him on the arm, give him a big smile. "Did she tell you I saw her today?"

"What? No… how—"

"See, she's already doing it. It begins.

Secret rendezvous, a warm chat about what might've been, a longing look and sweet words. I'm already in, and you can't do shit about it. I've been inside her. She's the mother of my child, for God's sake. You can't compare with me, not ever. But you go ahead and try. This will be fun."

"What is it with you? One minute you're on and on about protecting her, and the next you're ready to kill to get your way."

"If you only knew. Ask her about Donovan. She'll understand. Walk away, pretty boy, or it's going to get ugly. I'm done playing." I crack my knuckles. "And I won't hurt her. I'll hurt you, and everyone you ever loved." I see the challenge in his eyes, unspoken. He won't back off, and I don't blame him. She's worth dying for. Worth killing for.

May the best man win.

***

BROOKLYN

It's time. I'm in the parking lot of an attorney's office, unsure of why I'm so afraid to go inside. It's a big step, one I needed to do ages ago, but I guess I was afraid to take charge of things. Now I finally feel like I'm in a place where I can take control again, despite all of Cain's bullshit lately.

I hate to admit that it's because of Brandon, but it is. I feel like he's given me myself back—something I haven't had since I was a young girl in school, before Cain.

I need to be free of Cain, legally. Maybe if I can get him to agree to a divorce, he'll back off. I guess that's why I'm so worried, knowing that once he sees the papers, he'll lose his mind and probably come looking for me again, refusing to let me go.

There's no point in putting it off any longer, so I head inside. After paying a retainer, I talk to a lawyer and sign papers and all that other crap that comes along with being an adult. In the end, I'm told that I can't sell or destroy any assets, leave the area with Carissa, rack up further debt, or make threats. As if I would. But what I don't like is when the lawyer tells me that in Texas, there is no "legal separation," meaning we're still married and all our assets are community property, even things I gathered while he was in jail. He said in the end it'll be up to the judge, but everything I have can legally be split with Cain.

I nod and sign anyway, hating that he still has this hold on my life, even three years after we've been apart. He tells me Cain can contest, and if he does, we'll have to go to court.

I almost laugh. He *will* contest, there's no doubt. It's going to be a huge mess.

After I leave, I meet Ashley for lunch, a rare outing for us both. She's already at the little Mexican restaurant when I arrive, smiling at me as I flop into the seat and ask the waiter for an iced tea when I'd prefer a margarita. Too bad I have to work in a few hours.

"Well, I did it." I sigh, dipping a chip in green salsa.

"Did what?"

"Filed for divorce. I'm officially a grown-up."

"Oh, wow. Yeah, that's going to be a fun mess. Been there. But my ex didn't fight me. He gave me whatever I wanted to keep me from shouting from the rooftops what a low-life pervert he was." She rolls her eyes.

"That's what happens when your ex is a semi-famous fashion photographer." I dip another chip; suddenly my stomach is growling as if realizing how hungry I am for the first time. "I'm not so lucky. I hope he'll be lucid enough to just sign and let me go. I don't care if he takes everything I have. I just want him to go."

"Of course you do. Do you have any proof of the abuse? Did you ever take pictures or anything?"

"I wish I had something, but I don't. He has the DWI and then that short stay in the hospital recently, but that's all."

"It'll all work out. You're not alone. Speaking of that, how's Brandon? I hear he's just gaga over you." She grins at me.

I smile, pausing so we can place our orders when the waiter comes back.

"He hasn't told me he loves me again," I tell her. "It was just that one time."

"Well, he's probably just giving you space. I told you he was a good guy."

"Yes. you did. And he is. He's adorable and sexy and just totally amazing."

She leans forward. "Do you love him?"

I stuff a chip in my mouth, shrugging.

She laughs at my attempt to avoid the question. "Look, I know you have a lot going on, but nothing stops love. Especially when it's meant to be."

"Meant to be?" I echo. "This isn't a fairy tale."

"Who says?"

I roll my eyes, laughing at her. "What, the knight in shining armor saving the damsel?"

"What's wrong with that?"

I wave a chip at her. "I swore I wouldn't ever depend on a man for anything. I can save myself, when and if I need saving."

She nods. "Maybe you can, but what's wrong with letting him help?"

The waiter comes and refills our glasses, and I take a deep breath, not sure how to explain my feelings to someone who's never been in my shoes.

"Ashley, I just can't. I never stood on my own, not until you came along. First it was my parents, and then I went straight into life with Cain. He held me down, and for the longest time, I never thought I could take care of myself. He damn near brainwashed me into thinking I needed him or else I'd just flounder and die. Then when I finally left and was able to manage, keeping us alive, keeping Carissa from getting taken away or hurt despite the circumstances, I started to realize I could. I can. And I will. No matter if I love Brandon or not, something can always happen. If I end up on my own, I won't be left with nothing, with no way to care for her or myself, just because I'm in love with a good man who wants to rescue me."

She smiles. "So you do love him, then."

I grin. "Maybe."

Her squeal is too loud and turns heads, and I feel my face grow hot as I wave at the strangers eyeballing us. "Yay! Oh, I'm so happy for you. He's going to treat you like a queen, I just know it."

Queen. Not that I need that, but the thought makes me smile. Being spoiled sounds just heavenly.

"He tries now, but it's early, and all this drama is in the way, I think. I'm glad I listened to you."

"So am I. You should always listen to me. I'm always right."

I can't help but laugh, and it feels good to be lighthearted, if even for a short while.

The food arrives, and we dig in. After a moment, she starts up again.

"So, when are you going to tell him?"

I shake my fork at her. "Don't pressure me. It'll happen when it happens. He's not even pushing me. Damn, it's only been weeks. Some people wait a year to share that with the other person.""

"Yeah, but those are the people who don't really know what they feel, and they only say it because they figure it's been too long not to say it."

"That's probably true," I mutter into my plate. "Can we talk about something else?"

She shoves a forkful of food into her mouth. "Yes." Swallowing, she goes on. "Shane wants to have another baby. We've been talking about it."

"And?"

"And we're going to start trying."

My love life is forgotten as her eyes grow wider and a sparkle lights up her whole face, talking about her husband and babies.

We talk and talk, long after we've finished our meal, but eventually we have to say our goodbyes with the promise to have lunch together again soon. By the time I get home, I'm already exhausted. Regardless, I have to exercise; I can't let another day slip by. I mix up a pre-workout drink to give me a boost, then head to the bedroom to change.

As I'm opening the top to my shaker to take the first sip, I push open my bedroom door with my foot and find it dark. The curtains are drawn, the flicker of candlelight dancing on the walls. There are rose petals all over the floor and the bed, which has new white sheets and comforter, crisp and stark against the red of the petals.

I look around, searching for Brandon as my heart

dances in my chest. I spy a champagne bottle on the dresser, next to two glasses with sparkling golden liquid inside.

"If I'd been romantic, would it have made a difference?"

The voice behind me stops my heart and chills my blood. I turn only because I must. Cain's eyes are pleading, the lighter for the candles still in his hand.

He's blocking my exit.

I try to swallow, but my mouth is dry, my tongue sticking to the roof. I clutch my little shaker bottle to my chest as if it might shield me. "Cain, how did you get in here?"

"Does it matter? I'm here now. Would you have thought twice if I'd done more like this?"

"It's too late for questions like that." I force the words out of a dry throat, scanning the room for anything I might use as a weapon, should it come to that.

"It's never too late. We're still married, you know. Unless… have you cheated on me, love? Have you been with him?"

I see the warning flash in those dark eyes of his as he leans in the doorway, twirling the lighter. Sweat starts to roll down my back. "No, no, of course not," I lie.

He smiles. "Well, that's good. So, what do you think? Do you like it? I saw how you smiled when you walked in."

I glance around again.

The lamp? No, it's too far.
The champagne bottle. That might do.

I inch toward the dresser as I reply, hoping to distract him from my movements. "Cain, I don't understand you. Just the other day, you were here telling me to stay away, and now you're back trying to be romantic? What's going on?"

He nods as if he understands, then enters the room and closes the door, making sure to keep his body between me and it. "I realize you must be confused, but I still want you, Brook. I want *us*. And I need you to believe that I won't hurt you. I just want you to know I've changed. I want you to be safe, sound, and with me. You know I love you, don't you?"

I don't know how to respond. If I say what's on my mind, he might hurt me, and I have nothing but my wits to protect me against his 250 pounds, which has proven less than effective in the past.

I take in a breath and nod. "Yes, I know you do. The best way you know how."

He smiles and reaches for the champagne, handing me a glass. I take it, and he grabs the other. "To new beginnings, then."

I just stand there, trying to figure a way out of this. "I can't do this. You know I can't," I whisper.

He frowns, downing the drink, then takes mine and drinks that too. I glance at the bottle, but he grabs my hand and leads me to the bed, where we both sit down.

He reaches up and brushes my cheek, touches my

hair, gazes at me with soft eyes. "Well, maybe you need time. Maybe you need me to show you how tender I can be. I can be gentle, Brook. I know you think I'm a monster, but inside…." He lowers his head to my neck and breathes deeply. "You smell so good. You always did."

His lips graze my throat with a tenderness I haven't seen in him in years. His hand sinks into my hair, his mouth on my jaw, my ear. He turns my face and looks deeply into my eyes.

The worst part of the moment is that his touch doesn't make me sick, or ache, or even want him back. It just makes me sad. Sad that this man thinks he can be what I need just because he wants it. His need for me is genuine, but unfortunately, so is the twist in his temper.

"Don't you still feel it, baby? Isn't there something inside you that's still mine?"

My vision blurs with tears. I press my eyes closed to clear them, taking in a shaking breath. I feel his mouth on mine, slow and taking. I can't kiss him back, I just can't. It doesn't take him long to realize it, and he pulls away, eyes flashing. "You can't even try? For our daughter?"

Try for her? Is he kidding?

I pull away, out of reach of his touch, unsure of what to do, what to say. In moments like this, I've been forced facedown on my marriage bed, taken roughly against my will as I sobbed into a pillow. I find myself a bit paralyzed, fearing that may happen again if I don't tread carefully.

I thought the days of fearing rape were behind me. The tremble in my hands, the struggle to fill my lungs with a deep breath, and the sweat on my skin tell me I'm wrong.

So very wrong.

"Cain, it's been too long. Do you know what you did to me? Do you know how long it's been since you made love to me? Even before?"

He blows out a breath, leaning forward to rest his elbows on his knees. "Yes, I know. Don't you think I'm sorry for that?" There's an edge to his so-called apology.

"I don't know. How can you think 'I'm sorry' will make me forget it?"

He looks up into my eyes. His are pained. "I don't know. I just hope, I guess. I can't believe that after all our years together, all our firsts, you have nothing in you for me but contempt. I don't believe it. I never will."

You better, because that's all there is.

"I'm sorry. I won't ever hurt you again."

He means it, I'm sure. But it's just a promise he isn't capable of keeping. It's not in him to love gently.

"This can never be, Cain. I'm sorry. I know you want it to be, but it's too late." I steady myself, bracing as the next words come tumbling out. "I filed for divorce this morning."

His skin goes a shade lighter, and he gapes at me as

if the longer he stares, it might somehow make it not true.

"Cain, I'm sorry." My voice cracks, and after I say it, I realize I really am sorry. I said it just to calm him, but now I know the finality of this is painful all the way around.

"You're sorry? You didn't really, did you? You wouldn't. I don't believe it." He stands up and I shoot off the bed, backing toward the dresser.

"As soon as they get the documents prepared, they'll send them to you. I don't know where you live, but the lawyer told me not to worry, that they would find you," I ramble.

My heart thumps with every step he takes closer. My bedroom isn't that big, and he reaches me quickly, my back hitting the dresser. The bottle tumbles and tips, spilling champagne across the wood. "Was it his idea? It was, wasn't it? All this time, you never bothered, and all of a sudden you do this? It was him. I know it."

I shake my head. "No, I promise it wasn't. I was just scared before. He had nothing to do with it."

He bends close to my face. "I don't believe you. And I know you fucked him. I know you lied. I was willing to overlook it, but now I'm not so sure."

I have to tell my lungs to breathe. For a split second, I can't take in any air. *He's going to kill me this time.* His eyes darken right before me, just the way they used to. His pretty words are forgotten, as they always are once this part of him takes over.

Damn it, I shouldn't have told him.

"No, you're wrong. He's just my friend, that's all."

"You want to leave me so you can be with him."

I can't stop the tears now, or the shake in my voice. He reaches out and grabs my hair, making me gasp at the pain. "But I'm here with you. Not him."

He stops. His tight grip, one that's bruising my scalp, grows slack. "What do you mean, you're here with me? You just told me no. You told me—"

"I know. It's just been a long time."

"You're confused?"

I nod, sobbing.

"Tell me you love me," he says softly.

"Let me go, please."

And he does. He releases my hair and backs away. I turn and grab the bottle and a glass. I pour what little is left into it and realize I'm not thinking, just acting. I have no idea what I'm doing or what's about to happen.

"Tell me you love me," he says again, with more force this time.

"I loved you, once," I finally reply.

The back of his hand stings when it crosses my face, but I don't fall, years of leg workouts bracing me against it. The sharp tang of blood coats my tongue, and my lip swells instantly.

"You said you wouldn't hurt me again. You lied," I accuse, flipping the bottle in my hand so the heavy end becomes a weapon.

"I know. And you said you didn't cheat on me. So maybe we're even."

I wipe the blood on my sleeve, anger fueling me. "Get out of my house. I'll never love you again. I'll never let you touch me. I'll never be yours again. Fuck you."

When he raises his hand this time, I raise mine as well, but mine has a bottle in it. I break it over his head, and it staggers him. Blood and alcohol trickle out of his hair, and as he falls, dazed and sure to pass out, I turn and run.

Chapter Seventeen

CAIN

I WAKE UP ON THE FLOOR OF HER bedroom. The candles are out, but I can still smell the wax, so I know it hasn't been long. My head hurts, and it's sticky with the remnants of champagne and blood. When I sit up, the ache swells and I groan, gripping my head for relief but not finding it.

I wonder if she called the police. I almost hope she did. Maybe if I go back to prison, Donovan will leave me alone for the day or so I'm in custody. For now, he's hovering in the doorway, ready to rub all this in my face, I'm sure.

"What are you doing here?" I ask after a long silence. He finally steps into view with that smirk on his face. "Why are you always following me like some lost puppy? Don't you have your own life? Fuck, Donovan, go away. Go find some whore to bang and leave me to my own mess, will you?"

"Well, what am I supposed to do, just leave you to cry all over her and yourself? What woman wants a man like that? She wants a real man, one who will take charge. You let her walk all over you, kick your ass, and now she's gone again. You had her right where you wanted her. I thought you finally understood after our chat the other day."

I get up and head for the bathroom, washing my hands, my face. I'm not staying long enough to shower the rest of the blood out of my hair. It's on my shirt too, but I'll have to leave it for now. "I told you to stay out of this. Now I've hit her again, and she thinks I'm lying to her. That it's like it was before. How will I ever get her back if you don't leave it alone? Let me do things myself."

He laughs from his spot on the bed, shaking his head at me as I rub a wet towel through my hair, hoping to clean it out a bit. "You're like a pathetic little kid begging his mom for something. 'Mom, I can do it this time. I'll be good, I promise. I won't let you down,'" he mocks. "Aren't you pissed? Look at what she did. She's made a fool of you."

I stare at my reflection. "I am pissed." I'm pissed at him, at me. I hit her again. I didn't resist. I made her bleed, made her cry. "But she always forgave me before. She will again," I whisper to myself.

His laugh from the bedroom just makes me angrier. "Leave me alone. I don't need you anymore. Can't you see what you've turned me into?" I yell, picking up the larger piece of the bottle and throwing it at him. He dodges it easily enough, rolling his eyes at me.

"You're still a big pussy, if you ask me."

I cross the room and wrap my hands around his throat. His skin is cold. When I squeeze, he simply grins at me. "You can't kill me. You don't have it in you, remember?"

"But I can have fun trying, can't I?" I close my hands around his throat as tightly as I can, until all my muscles are clenched. I'm almost able to imagine him gasping for air, slapping at my hands, struggling, and then passing out. But none of that happens. He just smiles at me until I exhaust myself, but I don't say anything to him as I walk out, slamming the door behind me.

I drive to the same bar I hit last time, where I picked up that willing chick, Jessie or whatever her name was. Maybe a drink and a good lay will help clear my mind. When I get there, I switch my shirt out for a sweatshirt that's sitting on the seat beside me and go inside.

Maybe Donovan is right. Maybe all this fighting I'm doing isn't helping. What if I just give in and become what he wants? Though I don't even know what that is, because I thought I did it before, and yet he still made fun of me. No matter what, I'm not making anyone happy. Not Donovan, not Brook, not myself. I might as well do what I want once in a while. And tonight that is get shit-faced drunk and maybe laid.

In between drinks, I'll figure out my next move. I'm

not going to get anywhere with Brandon still in the picture. He has to go.

My threat plays in my head as I take my first slow sip of Jim Beam. The douche didn't believe me.

He won't be making that mistake next time.

I dial her number. I'm not a phone person—I like being face-to-face, so I avoid it—but desperate times, as they say. Of course, it rings and rings, no answer.

I decide to text her instead.

God, I'm so sorry. Are you okay? I know you hate me. If you could only understand what's going on. It's not me. It's him.

I hit Send, my heart empty and yet somehow heavy in my chest. I know she won't answer, but I can try. I can tell her how sorry I am.

***

BROOKLYN

My face throbs as I drive without knowing where I'm going.

Not home.

Not Ashley's.

The phone goes off beside me. Unknown number. I check the message and immediately know it's Cain. Of course it is. Blaming Donovan, like always. Nothing is ever Cain's fault.

I pull into a parking lot, my first instinct to ignore him. But where is that getting me? Nowhere. *Maybe if I face this head-on, just for a change.*

Me: What do you want? Oh yes, Cain, my love. I forgive you. For all the bleeding and bruises, the names, and all the times you raped me and laughed at me when I cried. I was silly to be so hateful to you. Please come running back to my arms, and we'll figure this out together. Ha, hardly. Go let your friend hold you until you feel better.

After I hit Send, I check my reflection and sigh. I thought I was past this—the bruised cheek, the swollen lip. I can hide some of it with makeup, but it won't help cover it all.

As I look at myself, the swell of shame washes over me. The thought that *I can't let anyone see I'm a victim. No one can know I've chosen to let him hit me.* It's all as fresh as this morning's coffee, like it just happened. The sickening feelings twisting my gut, the embarrassment that makes me run and hide, pretend my life is something it's not. Protecting him for it. Protecting myself, because no one can know I chose this.

I did choose this. The first time he hit me and I forgave him.

Then the next time.

And the time after that.

Of course he thinks I love him, that I'll come back. I always did. I made it him and us. This was our little private world, and no one knew but me and him. It was okay because I made it okay.

Hell, for all I know, everything he says is true. What if there really is some entity that's making him like this? How many millions of people believe in angels and demons and Heaven and Hell? I've never given it much thought, but then again, when you're trying not to be beaten to death on a daily basis, it's a bit distracting.

I need to talk to him, *really* talk to him.

My reflection mocks me. Talk to him? Who am I kidding? As if he's normal and can think and reason like a human being.

I shake the thought away and look around. I'm sitting in the parking lot of Brandon's office building. I don't remember coming here; I was just driving without thinking.

What is Brandon going to say? I know I have to tell him. I've never seen him get really angry, so I have no idea what sort of reaction I'm going to see. Protective? Is he going to storm out and kill Cain? Or will he just hold me and tell me he's sorry?

I don't even know which one I'd prefer. I don't want Brandon any deeper in this than he already is, but judging by the black-and-purple swelling on my face, I'm going to have to tell him something.

Maybe I can make something up. I used to be pretty good at that. Hiding behind makeup and lies, laughing it off—*oh, I'm such a klutz!*

Something akin to anger, maybe indignation, grows inside me. It swells and festers as I sit here in the silence, strangling the embarrassment, smothering the shame and the urge to lie about what happened.

I can't do this.

I can't slip back into that woman I was.

I'm strong now. I'm not her anymore.

I get out of the car and cross the parking lot. As I make my way inside the building and through the lobby, I draw a glance or two, a wrinkle of concern on a forehead here and there. When the elevator opens, I hit the button for his floor, then walk out once I reach my destination with my head high, as if this is where I belong.

And this *is* where I belong. I'm Brandon's now, and he's mine.

"Can I help you?" The receptionist's eyes dance across my face, then jerk back up to my eyes with a fake smile.

"I need to speak to Brandon Maradona. I'm his girlfriend, Brooklyn."

It's the first time I've let myself say it out loud. I've gone and labeled myself, and it makes me smile, then wince—smiling stings a little.

He picks up the phone, speaks to who I assume is Brandon, and then hangs up. "He said go on back, miss. He's the third door on the left."

I thank the man and head back, gripping my purse strap.

Brandon's office is neater than I expected. I always believed IT people's offices would be cluttered with electronic equipment and piles of wires and keyboards stashed on shelves. Of course, he's not an IT guy, per se; he's created software, so I suppose all his work is done on the computer itself.

Pride swells in my chest. He's smart, sexy, sweet, and mine.

And he's also rising from his desk with a growing look of concern that is melting his smile.

"Brooklyn, what in the world happened to you? Were you in an accident?"

Unexpected tears well in my eyes as I turn and close the door. "Um... I went home after my run this morning, and Cain was there. He'd set up candles and stuff in the bedroom for me, trying to... I don't know what. Long story short, I rejected him and pissed him off."

He comes around the desk, gingerly touching my face, turning it this way and that to examine me. "He did this to you? Are you hurt anywhere else?"

I shake my head, avoiding his eyes. That old feeling is coming back. "I broke a bottle over his head and left him unconscious on the floor."

He mutters something in Spanish, blowing out a breath. "Did you call the police?"

Funny, the thought never occurred to me. "No."

He raises an eyebrow at me. "Let's call them. Or I'll take you down there. That's probably better."

Instinct screams, *No, don't call! Leave them out of this,* but reasoning is a little louder. There's no reason not to call, not this time. I'm not hiding now. I'm not at risk of losing Carissa or anything else.

"I guess you're right. I should call them."

"Hey, are you okay? How are you feeling?" He grabs me, spinning me back toward him when I turn for the door.

Tears spill down my cheeks, and he wipes them off, love shining in his eyes mingled with anger. "I'm shitty, thanks for asking." I laugh through my sobs, and he smiles, pulling me into his arms.

"Baby, I love you. I'm sorry." His whisper curls around me like smoke, saturating me with lovely feelings and peace that soaks into my skin and cools the fire inside my soul.

I love him too. I can't say it, though I don't know why. I guess I just don't feel free yet.

***

A couple of hours later, I walk out of the police department and climb into Brandon's car feeling almost guilty. They said they'll most likely end up issuing a warrant for his arrest, and an emergency protective order will be issued that will prevent him from contacting me for up to ninety days. I don't know why I feel bad, because I shouldn't. I suppose that old love and the fact that he's the father of my child is what's doing it. I feel as if I've betrayed him.

"What?" Brandon puts a hand on my thigh, warming me through my jeans.

"What?" I echo.

"Why are you brooding over there?"

"Just thinking."

"About?"

I laugh. "Are we gonna do the whole 'what are you thinking' thing now?"

"You're avoiding the question." He glances at me, then back to the road.

I am.

"Wait, where are we going? You missed the turn back to your office."

"I know. We're going to your apartment to get your stuff. You're moving in with me."

"What?" I turn, twisting to look at him. "You—"

"I will fight you on this one, Brooklyn. You aren't going back there. He broke in, and he hit you. Get over your pride and suck it up. You're moving in, and that's final."

I open my mouth to retort, but nothing comes out. He's right. I can't go back. I can't go to Ashley's. He's found me every time.

"He might be following me," I mutter.

"He probably is. We'll trade cars."

"That won't work. He worked with you, so he might know yours too."

"True." He nods. "Wait, I have an idea." He takes a sharp left and heads out of town, then picks up his phone and places a quick call in Spanish.

* * *

"Where are we?" I ask as he pulls into the driveway of a nice little ranch-style brick home.

Brandon puts the car in Park. "This is my mom's house."

"What?" He's taken me to his mother's house. I sit in the car, looking down at my jeans and T-shirt—which still has blood on it—and my unmade reflection and cringe. Not a day to meet his mom. Not to mention the woman most likely won't want her son with someone who comes with baggage like I have. I'm not a safe, happy place for any man right now. I'm nothing but drama and danger. "Why now? Look at me. I'm not ready to meet your mother. We just started—"

"Stop. It's fine. You are stunning, and it will be fine."

"Brandon, are you insane?"

"We're trading cars. And yes, I probably am." He plants a swift kiss on my lips and then gets out. I just sit in the passenger seat, frozen.

He goes around and opens my door when he sees

I'm not following him. "What's the holdup?"

"I can't meet your mom like this. Look at me. And she won't like this. I realize what she must think about me. Any mom would."

He shifts his weight, cocking his head. "My mom isn't just any mom. If I love you, she loves you. End of story. And she can't wait to meet you. She's been asking me about it for a while now."

I swallow. "Come on, let's just go."

He shakes his head. "Nope."

I haven't met anyone's mother in… well, almost ever. "Just go alone. I'll wait."

He grins at me, holding out his hand. "Don't be nervous. She'll adore you. It's only a week till Christmas, and she was expecting you for that anyway."

Was she? Oh man, I didn't even think about that.

Giving in, I take his hand and he smiles at me. He has a lightness to his step as he drags me along that tells me he's excited. He wants her to meet me.

He's really proud to be with me.

I bite my lip, and he squeezes my hand. "Mama, I'm here," he calls, opening the door.

His mom pops into the living room with a smile just like his beneath blue eyes and blonde hair. She's a tiny woman, wiping her hands on a kitchen towel and rushing toward me with open arms.

"Encantado de conocerte. Eres tan encantador."

I find myself suddenly smothered in a hug by a woman who smells like perfume and coffee and spices, with no idea what she just said.

"English, Mama. Brooklyn, she says she's happy to meet you, and you're lovely."

"Yes, so very pretty. Come sit down."

"Mama, we need to talk to you. Brook has a problem, and I was hoping you can help." He launches into a cleaned-up version of my situation, light on the details. I sit quietly, growing hot with embarrassment, wishing I could vanish as they discuss me.

Mrs. Maradona looks at me with warm, motherly eyes and reaches for my hand. "You are right to come here. You are family now, if my son loves you. You are welcome here anytime. Don't worry, nothing will happen. Take my car, and use it as long as you like." She pats my hand. "Go get the keys, son."

"But it's dangerous," I squeak, not sure what to say or how to prevent her from getting involved. "I don't want anything to happen to you because of me."

"Hush, nothing will happen. You ask me for anything you need, you understand?"

I sigh and nod. "Okay then." Warmth comes off this woman like a light. She's nothing but love. Smiling, I thank her. What else can I do? She's just too sweet to refuse, and so very kind. Her heart is in her eyes, the same way Brandon's always is.

She releases me, then touches my face and smiles. "So beautiful. He told me all about you. Now, come sit down and tell me about yourself."

I glance over at Brandon, who is practically bouncing

in place. The man is obviously beyond happy that I've met his mother, and the love in his eyes is undeniable.

I feel my heart skip in my chest and my breath stutters. God, is this the moment when I finally realize I've met the love of my life, and he's standing here staring at me like I hung the stars in the sky?

His mom takes me by the hand and leads me into the kitchen. There is a pot of coffee on, and she guides me to a round breakfast table, patting the seat for me to sit down. Brandon moves to get us coffee, waving his mother off to go talk to me.

She's a lovely woman, and just a few minutes into the chat I adore her. No wonder Brandon is the way he is; with a mother like this, his whole family must be just amazing.

An ache for my own mother stirs, one I haven't felt for a long time. Memories of laughing and hugging, late-night chats with her, until I met Cain and everything went to shit.

I push the memories aside and refocus, answering her questions. She eventually comes to Cain and what happened, drawing a warning from Brandon, but she gives him the stink eye and he shuts up.

I grin. One look from his mom and he's a little boy again.

Oh God, I love this man.

I tell her the basics without including the gory details. She understands, and honestly, I don't think she wants to know. She quickly changes the subject, inviting us to stay for dinner. Brandon nods, saying he's called out for the rest of the day due to a family emergency. He offers to help her cook while I leave to go get Carissa, returning with her by the time dinner is ready.

My heart swells again at the idea that I'm his family emergency.

I watch her interact with my daughter, and I feel something I haven't felt for so long.

I'm family.

I haven't felt like part of a family in years, since I was a freshman in high school. Now, sitting with Brandon's whole family—his twin brother, wife, and kids came for dinner as soon as they heard I was here—I feel like I am.

I belong somewhere again. I'm home.

Chapter Eighteen

CAIN

THE DIVORCE PAPERS BURN MY HAND AS if they're on fire. The receptionist eyeballs me as I shift in my chair, unable to sit still.

Fucking bitch. I can't believe she did it.

"Believe it, you idiot. It's your own fault. You let her get away. You let her go way too far without pulling her back in. Now you've all but lost her," Donovan says quietly from beside me in the otherwise empty waiting area.

"I haven't lost her. I won't lose her."

"You have divorce papers in your hand, dumbass. She knocked you out when you tried to seduce her."

"It won't be over until one of us is dead."

"So you aren't going to give up? Watch him ride off into the sunset with his dick in her? Sit and cry like the little bitch you are?"

Donovan's taunts threaten to make me lose my

resolve, right here in this waiting room. I swallow, craving a smoke and a drink to dull the throb that's starting in the back of my head.

"No, I'm not. I'm never going to let him have her."

"Good."

I'm called into a hallway with thick carpet under my feet and the scent of highly fragranced candles burning somewhere unseen, then ushered into an office. It's all windows and a huge desk with an attorney sitting behind it, smiling and waving at us to take a seat while still on the phone.

Prick.

"Mr. James. What can I do for you?" he says once he hangs up.

I stand up and place the papers on his desk. "You're my wife's attorney. You sent me these papers. I want you to turn down the case."

He glances down at the documents, then back up at me with laughter in his eyes. "Mr. James, I'm sure you understand that this isn't the first time this has happened to me. I'm sorry for your circumstances, but you must realize that I can't do that."

"I'll pay you."

"I'm sure you would, but like I said, I can't do that. I suggest you get your own attorney."

I lean over his desk. "Look, you don't know who you're dealing with here. I don't want to see anything happen to you, so I suggest you just let this one go. It's not going to be worth it for you in the end if you don't."

Donovan walks up behind me. I shake my head at him, but he simply smiles at me, circling the desk and cracking his knuckles.

The lawyer's smile and cocky smirk vanish.

"Really, I'm here for your own good," I add.

"You need to leave. I'm going to call security."

Donovan places his hands on the man's shoulders.

"Don't do it. You're causing me too much trouble," I say to Donovan.

"I'll protect you. I always do, don't I?" Donovan looks up, meeting my eyes with his light ones.

"No, you don't. I was in prison for three years, and you didn't do shit to protect me."

The lawyer's face goes ashen.

"My friend here, he wants to kill you."

His face pales further as he stands, looking over his shoulder.

"Just drop the case and he won't hurt you. Just call her and tell her you can't take it on right now. I'm really here to protect you. You must understand."

"Get out. Please just go," the lawyer pleads. "I won't take the case. I'm not going to deal with… this. I'll have my secretary call your wife."

Relief floods me. She'll have to find a new lawyer, which will give me time to change her mind.

"Call her now."

He picks up his phone and addresses his secretary. "Beth, call Mrs. Brooklyn James and advise her that we won't be able to take her case. Tell her we'll cut her a check for the retainer, and she can come pick it up at her convenience."

He hangs up and stares at me. "There. Can you please leave now?"

"Yes, of course. And thank you."

I grab my papers and turn for the door. A crack followed by a sickening crunch and the thump of a heavy body hitting the floor stop me in my tracks.

I close my eyes. I don't want to look.

But I must.

Donovan is standing over the man's lifeless form, now just a well-dressed corpse on the floor.

"Damn it, why did you do that?"

"For fun. He's a lawyer. They lie. You really think he's going to refuse the case?"

"But he did!"

He rolls his eyes. "Please. As soon as you leave, he would've called her back. Let's go. You're such a pussy. God, I have to do everything for you, don't I?"

I turn, rushing out of the office before we're seen yet knowing it's too late. I had an appointment; all the cops have to do is look at the books. Too many people saw me come in here. It's only a matter of time now.

"What are you doing to me? You want me to end up in jail?" I rant in the elevator.

Donovan just smiles, reaching out to pat my cheek. "Poor, poor baby. So untrusting. No faith. Just wait and see. I'll take care of everything. Why must you always doubt me?"

It's easier to believe him than it is to argue, so I fall against the wall, watching his smiling face and pale eyes. I have to believe in something, in someone.

He's all I have, all I've ever had. What other options are there?

"Okay, so what do I do now?"

He nods, moving to put an arm around me just as the doors open. "Now it's time to make good on that threat to lover boy. You know he hasn't been taking you seriously."

I swallow, my voice trembling when I admit, "I was hoping I was wrong about that. She really is sleeping with him, isn't she?"

An old man gives me a weird look. I wink at the old fart, and he turns away, clearly embarrassed.

* * *

BROOKLYN

It all just kind of happened. The day with his family, then me confessing my real feelings in the throes of hot sex. I ended up telling him that I love him. It just slipped out, but the look on his face and the feeling I had after saying it made me sure that I did the right thing.

When it was out, it was such a relief, like a boulder was lifted off me. One less load that I didn't realize I was carrying. My burdens are so many that I don't notice them anymore, but now I realize most of them are my own doing. Things I just refuse to put down and let go of.

I moved out of my apartment, and Brandon insisted on paying to store my stuff that didn't fit at his place. It was the first place we had on our own, me and Carissa. It got us where we needed to be, but now Brandon is home.

He said having me move in for good was the best gift I could've given him for Christmas. He and I even took Carissa to the store to get whatever she wanted to decorate her new bedroom.

I took her to lunch on Christmas Eve, and we had a talk. I ended up explaining to her that Brandon wasn't ever going to replace her real dad, but her real dad has some problems, and it means he's not around. I made sure she understood that it has nothing to do with how much he loves her. Despite how much I loathe the man, I know my child needs to know he loves her, even if he is a monster. As much as I'm tempted to just let her hate him, I don't want to poison her heart that way. In the end, she would just hate me for that, and I can't bear that thought.

I have a family now, one beyond just me and my girl against the world. Now she has a sister, and a real father figure, and a grandmother, as well as the rest of

Brandon's family.

When Christmas morning arrives, magic is thick in the air. I don't remember a Christmas like this since my childhood. Watching the girls with their gifts from Santa, the bittersweet emotions as Carissa opens the ones from her father, all while asking if she'll see him today.

God, I hope not.

Brandon got me a diamond necklace and tons of clothes. He went crazy, and he's absolutely thrilled about it, judging by the look on his face.

"I only got you the watch. I feel like I didn't do enough now." I fake a pout.

"Are you kidding? You moved in. You're mine. That's all I wanted anyway."

That afternoon, we have Christmas all over again at his mom's house, with more gifts and more food, watching Christmas movies, and getting a little tipsy on the wine. We celebrate long into the evening, until the kids fall asleep and Brandon is nuzzling me on the couch, whispering to me that he wants to go home and take me to bed.

I agree, and we scoop up the kids, the gifts, and I give his mom a hug. "Thank you so much," I say.

She laughs in my ear, pulling back to take my face in her hands. "You are happy?"

"Yes. So happy. It's been so long."

She kisses my forehead, the way only a mother can, and hugs me again. "Good. You are my family now. Good night."

***

CAIN

The little house is nice. One-story, well-kept little brick home, lit up by security lights in the yard and the light of the full moon high overhead.

It's a shame to have to do this. But I warned him. I warned them both.

I suck on the cigarette, cracking the window to let some of the smoke out.

In the end, I'm doing this for her. She'll know. She'll understand that my love for her is everything, even when it comes to this. No one will ever love her like me.

She won't ever be able to doubt it, not now.

The smell of the gasoline in the trunk is making my head hurt. I glance over at Donovan, who's riding shotgun. "You sure this is the right thing?"

He rolls his eyes at me. I knew I shouldn't have asked. "Are you kidding? You told the SOB if he didn't back off, you would do something. If you don't keep your word, then what are you? You're a joke. They're probably in bed right now laughing at you. Is that what you want?"

Visions of her on all fours, him deep inside, pulling her hair as she moans, fill my mind. My blood heats up, and suddenly it's too hot in here, despite the chill in the air. Anger comes off me like smoke, because now all I can see is her with his dick inside her.

"No, that's not what I want. I guess you're right. This is unavoidable."

I get out of the car, glancing around. It's about 2:00 a.m. No one in sight. Donovan grabs the gas can, and we head for the door. He picks the lock with ease, making me wish I'd learned to do that myself.

Inside, the house is dark, but it still feels homey. The Christmas tree is on, bright multicolored lights dancing around and around, glancing off the little knickknacks that fill the shelves of the old woman's house.

Brandon's childhood home.

The smell of gas becomes nauseating as he starts to douse the tree, the floor, the couch.

"You think she'll wake up?" I glance up, noting the smoke detector in the hall. I reach up, pulling it down with one jerk and removing the battery.

"Who knows? Who cares? He'll learn not to fuck with you. Once this is over, you'll have to get her back, teach her not to be a whore. You know that, right?"

I start to open my mouth. *She's not a whore.* Instead, I walk farther down the hall, into the open bedroom of the older lady who lives here. His mom. Close to the door is another smoke detector; I give it the same treatment, pocketing the battery. She snores lightly but never stirs.

"Come on, let's go."

I follow him back toward the front door. I probably missed one or two more, but I'd kind of like to give the old broad a fighting chance. I toss my cigarette toward the tree, and it catches in an instant. The fire is beautiful, alive, dancing and breathing as it spreads to the curtain, chasing the trail of the gas across the carpet to the couch.

The air rapidly becomes unbreathable, forcing me out into the yard.

He won't fuck with me now.

I've never started a fire before, so sitting in the distance and watching is too much to resist. It doesn't take as long as I expected for the house to go up, fully engulfed in flames that both give life and take it away.

After a while, fire engines sound in the distance, and I've yet to see the old lady come out of the house. Regret forms like a hard ball of stone in my gut, realizing what must be happening inside. Never waking up, smothered in the smoke before the flames reach the bed.

I hope she didn't wake up. I don't want to think about the alternative, what I might've done to someone who likely didn't deserve it.

The fire trucks come and fight the flames for hours. In the end, when the sun is starting to turn the sky soft shades of yellow and purple as it rises for the day, they bring the body out. She's on a gurney, covered in cloth. Dead.

I lit the fire. I killed that woman. I can't put this one on Donovan—it was all me. I just hope Brook will forgive me and know I had to do it for her. Everything I do is for her. She knows that by now.

Pulling out my phone, I type a quick text.

I love you.

I hit Send, leaving it simple. She knows—she always did. Even after all this fighting, this anger, this rage, the hate in her eyes. It's just the game we play. In the end, she'll look up at me and smile, take my face in her hands, and tell me it's always been me. And I'll forgive her, and she me, and we'll be us again.

Chapter Nineteen

CAIN

THIS HAS GOTTEN OUT OF CONTROL. He's out of control. I sit in my apartment, staring at the news report. The old woman died. What was I thinking, following him there and setting the fire?

But I had to do something, didn't I? Brandon had to know I meant business. He had to understand that she's not his.

She's mine. Always will be, no matter what.

I have to get to her. Last time was a disaster, but I have to do something.

I just don't know what.

The gifts didn't work. The romance didn't work. Begging hasn't worked.

But there is one thing I haven't tried.

I swallow a mouthful of whiskey and hit Rewind on the DVR, playing the news report again.

If she knows, she'll let him go. If she realizes what's

coming, she'll come home.

You can't let him father your child. You can't let him take your family away, no matter the cost.

His warning echoes all around me. Donovan's right. I can't let that happen, and I know he *won't* let that happen.

* * *

The club where she works always has a line outside to get in and is always crowded. One of those places you have to dress to go to, not like the dive bars I've been frequenting.

Knowing what will happen if I go inside, I wait out here. After midnight, I use a slim jim and break into the car she's been driving. They thought they could fool me with a different car, like I'm an amateur. I've been doing this for way too long for these weak maneuvers.

Turns out it's his dead mom's car. Neat, no clutter. I crawl into the back seat and slouch down, eyes on the door.

She has to come out eventually.

* * *

BROOKLYN

The night is going well, and the club is packed. My phone starts ringing in my pocket, and I smile when I take it out and see Brandon's name lighting up the screen.

"Hey, baby. How are you?" I purr into the phone.

"Um, can you come home?" He sounds like he's been crying. My blood runs cold.

"What's wrong?" I stop walking in the hall just outside my office. "Are the girls okay?"

"Yeah, the kids are fine. They're here. But I just… just try and come home, please?"

"I'll see what I can do."

He hangs up without another word.

Worried, scared, my mind racing, I get permission to leave and walk out the door. I sit in Brandon's mom's car for a moment after getting in, scared of what I'm going home to.

"Don't scream. I have a gun."

The deep voice comes from the back seat, and I freeze. *Christ, this again.* I blow out a breath, palming my keys and turning to him.

His face is shadowed in the darkness, but the dim light reflects off his blue eyes. "You never give up." I sigh.

"No, I never will. I need to talk to you."

"I have nothing left to say to you. Let me see the gun."

He holds up the weapon, the one he took from me.

I breathe deeply and look back into his eyes. "I'm listening."

"I thought you might. You have to come home now, Brook. This party is over."

I don't say anything. How can I? He has a gun on me, and I know how easily he can go off the rails.

"Here's the thing. I can't control Donovan anymore. I'm not sure I ever did, really. In the past, he always listened to me, but now he's just doing what he wants because he thinks I've lost control. I guess I have, but you need to know what he's done."

A slow chill creeps into my veins, the ominous tone in his voice making me afraid. I swallow thickly, glancing down again. "What's happened?"

"He's killing people, Brook. I can't seem to get him to stop." He shakes his head, then looks out the window. "I don't want anyone else to die."

Fuck.

I shift in the seat. "Who, Cain?"

"The priest. The lawyer. My mom. Brandon's mom. I had no control over him. I still don't."

I feel sick.

Four people. Dead.

"You killed four people? You killed Brandon's mom?" I can't keep the squeak out of my voice. *That's why Brandon called me, why he's crying. Oh God. Such a wonderful woman.* Tears fill my eyes, but I push back the emotions, steeling myself.

Cain leans forward, moving between the bucket

seats with his elbows up. "No, not me. Donovan. I watched him. I was there, but it was him. I didn't want anyone to die. I mean, I knew his mom might die, but he wasn't listening to me." He pauses for a second. "There is one other thing, Brook."

I meet his eyes, dread building in my stomach, along with the need to vomit.

"He won't let my child be raised by another man. He thinks he has my best interest at heart. We can't let that happen, you know that, right?"

I can't move. Terror creeps into the car, hanging between us, curling around me like a physical entity.

"He'll kill her before that happens. I can't let him kill my baby. My little girl. You can't let that happen."

I choke down the bile in my throat, leaving a bitter taste in my mouth. "What do I do?"

"You have to come home. It's the only way."

Come home. God, no. Not this. He's going to see to it that my baby is killed if I don't come back to him.

I lean back, shaking. Cain reaches for me, and I try to jerk away, but there's nowhere to go in this small car.

"You understand now, don't you? You have to leave him. You have to come back. I'll forgive you for cheating on me, and we can start over. I'll take care of you this time, baby. I promise. But you have to come back, or she'll die. He'll kill her, and maybe you too. I don't want him to hurt you, and I don't know how to make him go away."

Tears roll down his face, and now mine too.

"Please, I can't watch you die. I can't watch my baby girl die and be buried. Please don't make me."

I can't hold it back anymore. All I've run from, everything I've put behind me is back in my face, pulling me back in. I have no options now. I can't let him kill Carissa. My child is my life.

I bend over and vomit all over the passenger seat, emptying my lunch and the drink I had onto the upholstery.

"Cain, please don't do this. Please," I beg, wiping my mouth on my shirt.

"It's not me. It's him. I can't make him stop. I've asked him to leave me alone, but he won't do it. I'm stuck. But we can make the best of it. We can be a family, be happy. If we're happy, he'll leave me alone. He'll leave us alone, I know it. He won't have a reason to stay anymore."

His eyes shine with desperation. Eager for me to say yes, terrified I'll say no and he'll have to do the unthinkable.

"Did all those people really die?" I whisper.

He nods. "Yes. I watched him break my mom's neck. He hanged the priest, and the lawyer—your lawyer—he snapped his neck too. You have to come back to me. Tonight."

"I can't. Not tonight. Carissa… my job… my stuff. I need more time." I blink away tears, a lump stuck in my throat.

Everything hurts. I escaped this. It was over. This can't really be happening to me. I'm going to wake up, and this will be another one of my nightmares.

Cain eyes me, as if contemplating what I've said. "Fine. You have forty-eight hours. I can hold him back if I tell him you're packing up, ending things. But then you have to meet me, or he'll do it. It's out of my hands. You know that, don't you?"

I nod. "I know that's what you believe. I believe you, Cain."

The stink of vomit is making my stomach ache again.

End things with Brandon. Go back to live with Cain.

"I can't be held responsible for what may happen if you don't show up. And you know if you run, we'll find you."

There's no running now. It's too late for that. I have two days to end my life as I know it, or I get to watch my daughter die. Surely he's lost what's left of his mind if he thinks I'm going to risk my life and hers to go back to that hell.

Silence hangs between us for the longest time. I can't think, can't settle my mind on one thought. It's too much to take in: absorbing this threat, the murders he's just told me about, and what my next move might be. Lives depend on it, and I can't even think.

He reaches out and takes my hand, and this time I don't jerk away. He runs his thumb across my skin, then bends and kisses my fingers. I feel nothing, numbness settling in to protect me, I suppose.

Looking up, I meet his gaze. "Where do I meet you?"

* * *

I'm not going back. I kick him out of the car, watching him drive away with no idea what my next move is. I have to get him out of my life, out of Carissa's life.

But if I don't go back, he could kill her. I can't put my happiness above her life. I never have before, and I can't start now.

I pull into a twenty-four-hour car wash and attempt to clean out the inside of the car. Of course, it doesn't really do anything. I head home, leaving the window down after I sprinkle a box of baking soda inside to absorb the vomit, and hopefully the smell.

He told me what happened. I can call the police; if I tell them, surely they'll investigate. Maybe if they look into it, they'll find something and get him off my back.

By the time they find something, we may all be dead. That's too much to risk.

When I get home, my mind is in a fog. The kids are asleep while Brandon and his brother sit on the couch, both of them with puffy, red faces. They break the news to me, and I cry with them—for her, for me, for the life I fell in love with that I might lose the day after tomorrow. But I don't tell them. I just sit up, I make coffee, I hold him and help him make phone calls and arrangements.

It's late when his brother leaves. Brandon finally passes out next to me, but I can't sleep. I thought my insomnia was gone, but now it's laughing at me as I lie wide awake, unable to shut my brain down. It's just too much.

Instead of going to bed, I sit at the kitchen table with the laptop and start searching.

I find the obituary for my lawyer easy enough. The details aren't there regarding his death, of course, but he's dead just like Cain said.

Nauseated again, I hold my head in my hands. How has it come to this? Murder? God, I should've gotten him help somehow. I should've made it happen.

He mentioned a priest, but seeing that I have no idea what he's talking about, I don't know where to look. Why was he talking to a priest anyway? Seeking help? I close the computer and stare into the darkness. Sleep won't be finding me anytime soon.

I'm sure Brandon is upstairs, unaware of any of this, sleeping soundly. Do I tell him? Do I do this on my own? If I drag him any further into this, he'll end up dead too. If Cain or Donovan or whoever isn't above killing a child, then Brandon isn't safe with me. That leaves me only one option, but how to do it? Just vanishing is the easiest way, but he'll look for me.

I could leave a note, I guess. Maybe if I explain, he'll just let me go and realize it's for the best.

Sometimes we just can't get what we want. Some people just aren't meant to be happy.

My stomach churns and my chest hurts. My happiness, her life. His life. They'll still be alive, but at what cost? Seeing him hit me, what kind of man will she end up with? What sort of woman will she grow into?

Of course, there is one other option.

Be smarter. Cain trusts me, even now. He thinks he's a victim in this, just like I am. Donovan's victim. He thinks it's me and him against Donovan, and together we can get rid of him once and for all. Maybe I can use that trust against him. Get him to open up, get something on him, and get him thrown into prison once and for all. There won't be any getting out of jail in Texas after killing four people—not alive, anyway.

But Brandon, he's going to be crushed. Somehow, he's going to have to trust me. Trust that I'm smart enough, strong enough, and that I'll be back.

Am I? Can I pull this off? Bunk with a killer, play house? Be the loving wifey, all the things Cain's always wanted and expected from me?

Means to an end.

Everything ends. Nothing goes on forever.

I look back at the computer, clearing the browser history before shutting it down.

Will Cain believe it? That after all this time, I've changed my mind and am ready to give him a chance to try again?

I turn off the light in the kitchen, making my way toward the bedroom, memories of all our past fights flashing through my mind one after the other.

I forgave him every time. He cried and begged, and I forgave him. He probably thinks this is just one long fight, and I'm finally over my mad spell.

Brandon is asleep on his stomach in bed, the blankets at his waist, his bare, muscled back moving with every deep breath he takes. My last night with him. Maybe forever. Who knows how this will end? If it comes down to depending on the police to come and take him away? Never really dependable, always a risk.

But it's a risk I have no choice but to take. I hope I'll be able to come back to him. I've never been as happy as I have been with him. Now I'm going to have to let him go.

Tears form in my eyes, standing here in the dark. I know I won't be sleeping, but I strip down to just panties anyway and crawl into bed. Brandon moves, wrapping me in his arms, pulling me into his body, skin on skin. He nuzzles me, half asleep, not really awake enough to know what he's doing. I stare into his face, his beautiful, passionate features that always have a smile, always ready for a kiss. Lips that caress my name the way no one else's ever have.

My tears slip onto my pillow. I close my eyes, pressing my face into his chest, absorbing him. His scent, this feel, the sound of his breathing, and the way he makes me feel so delicate against his larger body.

I can't believe I found love, real love, in all this. I almost wish I never had. It would be easier than lying here crying because I have to go, returning to a level of hell that I thought I'd left far behind me.

The next morning, nothing unusual happens. Brandon leaves me with a kiss on my forehead, thinking I'm sleeping. I have to get up to take Carissa to school, but I lie here for a moment longer. Eventually I rise, a terrible dread in my gut as I smile at him, rushing around as we get the girls ready for school and he gets ready for work. Eventually we part ways, and when I get back, when the place is empty, I stand for a long time in the middle of the room, struggling to prepare myself for what's coming. *Might as well get it over with.* I spend the morning packing up, removing any trace of us that I can find from the house. When that's done, it's past lunchtime.

The last thing I do is sit down with a pen and paper.

Chapter Twenty

CAIN

PART OF ME WANTS TO BELIEVE MORE than anything that she's finally coming around, but the other part is sick with worry. When I said Donovan would kill her, I'm afraid it was true, not just a scare tactic. Death seems to means nothing to him.

I haven't seen him since before yesterday when I laid it all out for Brooklyn in the car. I told him if I did it, he would have to leave me alone for a while. I need time alone with my family, with Brook. She still hates me, I see it in her face, but I know she'll forgive me like she always did. It's not in her to hate. She's too good for that.

Besides freaking out, I've spent the last few hours getting ready. I bought us a house with cash, a process I started before Christmas, hoping I might get the chance to surprise her with it. I had to get furniture ordered, things moved, pay moving guys, and pack up and leave this shitty apartment. I haven't heard from her all day, but she said she'd come. I don't think she'll risk it—at least I hope she won't. I just don't know how to hold him back anymore.

It's just past three when my phone rings. I've been putting together shelves for Carissa's room for the last hour. I set the screwdriver down and pull out my phone, surprised and almost scared to see my wife's name lighting up the screen.

"Hello?"

"Hey. Um… are you… where are you?"

"I'm here at home. Why?"

"Oh. Um… well… can we come now? I don't want to go back to the house and risk having to face Brandon. I just picked her up from school and told her what's going on."

My heart beats hard in my chest. Her voice is clear, not crying like it was last night. She's sure. I can't hear any hint of doubt now. I knew she would get over it eventually. "Yeah, yeah. I've been getting things ready all day. It's not perfect, but I haven't had enough time," I ramble, standing up.

"That doesn't matter. Cain, you and I have to talk. Really talk. Can we do that? Maybe tonight after she goes to sleep?"

"Yeah, I guess we do need to talk. Are you ready for the address?"

"Yes."

I rattle it off, then have her repeat it to be sure she

got it right.

She sighs into the phone. "We'll be there in a few minutes." She hangs up.

The next few minutes are spent getting the boxes and trash out of the house and piled up in the garage, and just trying to get things as nice as I can for her. She has to see how sorry I am. I should've done this for her years ago, instead of gambling everything away and putting her up in a shithole of a rented hovel. Now she'll have a nice house, and I'll take care of her.

She pulls up in a taxi, which surprises me. "Where's your car?" I ask as she takes bags out of the back.

"It burned up at Brandon's mom's. It was in the garage. I've been in her car, but I can't take that with me. It's not mine." She pays the driver as Carissa stands beside her, holding a purple My Little Pony backpack in one hand and waving at me with the other.

"Oh, well, I have one. You don't need it anymore." I move forward, taking bags from her.

She turns, looking up at me. "I have a job, Cain."

"You can quit. I'm taking care of you, remember? You don't need to bust your ass taking care of strangers."

"I like my job." She frowns.

"You'll adjust."

She swallows, looking away. We both glance down at our daughter, who seems happy but a bit confused.

"Baby, do you like the house?" I ask, bending down to scoop her up. She nods and wraps her little arms around my neck. Brooklyn takes in a sharp breath at the sight but doesn't say anything.

"Whose house is this?" Brook asks. "Did you rent it?"

"No, I bought it. Let's go inside."

She stops walking. "How did you buy it? You don't even have a job. You got fired."

"Cash. I inherited money from my dad when he died."

She frowns at me. "He died a year before you and I split up."

"Yeah, I hid the money. I didn't want to blow it all on… well, never mind on what."

She grabs my forearm when I start to walk again, stopping me. Her hand is warm on my skin. It's the first time she's touched me voluntarily.

"Wait a minute. You had money hidden from us? We lived on the streets. I almost starved to death. I still have trouble sleeping at night from it."

"Yeah, but I didn't know that. My mom had the money, and I talked to her about that after I got out. I told her she should've called me, that I would've taken care of you. I never wanted that for you two."

"You talked to her? But she's…."

I nod. "Yeah, Donovan. Not me. If I'd known what was going on, I would've taken care of it."

She takes in a breath, her eyes watering, but she blinks it away. "You would've taken care of it? Cain, you were the reason it even happened."

I look at Carissa, who's frowning at the pair of us. "I know. We'll talk about this later, okay? Let's get inside and look at our new house, order some pizza, and get settled."

Brooklyn lowers her head, nodding in agreement. We can't do this in front of Carissa; she's too old now and would figure out what's going on.

Just before we cross the threshold of the house, I grab Brooklyn's hand and turn her toward me, her brown eyes meeting mine. They're defeated.

"Brook, this is a new start for us. We'll begin again. But you have to remember not to push me, you know? Please, just don't push me. You know where my buttons are, but just don't."

For a long, cold moment, we just stare at one another, until finally she nods. "I know. Let's go inside. It's getting chilly out here. I think a cold front is coming in tonight."

***

Brandon,

I feel that saying I'm sorry is nothing but a cliché, but I am. This isn't what I wanted. None of this is what I wanted. Maybe I should've just told you face-to-face, but with Cain on my back, I worry about the lives of those I love and how much danger I'm putting them in.

I do love you. I adore everything about you. You made

me me again. You allowed me to flourish once again, to grow past what my fear turned me into and become a person once more. I'll also say this—if I'm not allowed to love you the way I want to, then I'll never love anyone again. I meant it when I said you were the end of the line for me. You are.

Now I guess I should tell you what happened. Cain broke into my car last night. When I got off work, I found him sitting in the back seat waiting for me. He told me Donovan is out of control and has killed four people. I sat there and listened to him tell me about a priest, my lawyer, his mom, and your mom, how they all died at Donovan's hand and how he can't control him anymore. Then he told me that they can't let another man raise Carissa, and that Donovan threatened to kill her if I didn't walk away. He told me the only way to protect her was to come home.

When I got home, I looked it up online, and people actually are dead. He said Donovan broke his mom's neck and hanged the priest. Said he didn't really want your mom to die, but he lit the fire, how he didn't have a choice. I have no options. I couldn't risk her life then, and I won't now. I can only hope that I can get something on him by earning his trust and playing the loving wife. Then I can get him locked up for good and out of my life so I can come home to you again.

Maybe since you're a father, you can understand. I'd imagine you would risk your life to protect Ava. I must protect her, but I feel like I've brought her to the mouth of the beast to keep her from being eaten. Living here won't do her any good, so I have to get what I can on him and do it fast.

Don't come looking for me. It'll only get you—and maybe me—killed. If anything happens to me, please find Carissa and find a way to protect her. I know you're not legally able to take her, but somehow maybe you can be there for her and love her and be a second father so she can have a healthy relationship with a dad in her life. Keep her safe if I'm gone, please.

And whatever happens, know that I do love you, and I'm trying to make it back to you.

Love,

Your Brooklyn

***

BROOKLYN

I don't know what I'm doing. I'm just going through the motions, reminding myself that I'm here to save her, save us, and get him out of the picture. I have to find something, but how long will that take?

He has to trust me, but unfortunately, I'm just not sure how good an actress I am. Time will tell, I guess.

The house is gorgeous, as much as I hate to admit it. He listened to me, all those years ago when we were kids and I would talk about the house we would live in someday. He went out and found it, the bastard. Trying to win me back. He said he's ordered furniture, showed me pictures of breathtaking pieces. A leather living room set that looks like it's made of butter that might melt in the sunlight. A bedroom set that's to die for—dark wood, four-poster bed with feathery fine linens. A white canopy bed for Carissa, shelves for her toys, a desk to do homework on. He's gone all out. But when I ask him how much money his dad left him, he won't tell me. He says I don't need to worry about the money, that he'll handle it.

I swallow, nodding in agreement while biting back my sarcastic comments. I used to handle the money the first time around. I'd freak out because he'd gamble, drink, and fuck away his paycheck and leave me nothing to pay the rent with. We would fight, and he would win. I sold my wedding rings and anything else of value to keep us afloat. God knows he wouldn't let me work. When I went out once and found a job working as a waitress in a diner down the road, he locked me in the closet for days, telling me I had to learn my place and I'd become too "cocky."

I never did that again.

I try to busy myself, because if I sit, I'll flip the fuck out. I move things around, unpack, direct the delivery men when they arrive with the bed. I wash the dishes—hell, I even go to the garage and hook up the washer and dryer, then put on a load of laundry. I play with

Carissa, read to her, anything to keep busy.

But night falls, and she needs a bath, needs to get her rest. I wash her, then tuck her in. I watch as Cain kisses her forehead and reads to her, stroking her little face as her eyes grow heavy, telling her he loves her so.

He does love her, and it hurts me to see it. This is a man who's never known gentle love. He has no idea what to do with his feelings, but he's trying. I see he's really struggling to be better. But then when he stands, turning his blue eyes on me, I'm reminded of all the times in the past that he "tried."

He failed then, and therefore he'll fail again. He always does. He always will. A leopard can't change his spots, as they say.

With the only thing standing between him and me asleep, my fear grows by the moment, rising in my throat like bile and choking me as we tiptoe out of her new princess bedroom, closing the door behind us.

I miss Brandon, so much that my eyes burn with unshed tears. My throat hurts from the lump forming, so I duck into the bathroom and tell Cain I need to shower. I lock the door, strip down, and stand under water as hot as I can stand it. My skin burns and turns pink as I sink to the floor under the spray, holding my knees and sobbing like a baby.

There's no one to hold me now, no one to tell me it's okay. To say Brandon will understand, that he'll know I did it because I had to. Instead, I imagine that he hates me. Cursing my name, burning the letter, going to the bar and picking up a willing woman to fuck away my memory, washing it all down the drain and leaving him to go love another.

He's not that man. I know he's not, but under these kinds of circumstances, when people are hurt and angry, who knows what they'll do? The darkness of the human mind, the black spot that sits on every human soul only festers with pain and wrongdoing, growing just a little larger every time. He's no exception. None of us is.

I hear the doorknob rattle as he tries it. Some clicking sounds follow, and then the door opens. I stand from my spot in the corner of the shower, running my face under the water to hide my tears before grabbing the shampoo.

Bastard unlocked it. So much for a moment of privacy.

"Brook, why did you lock the door?" I see his blurred shape through the glass shower door.

"It's a habit," I lie.

"You've been in here a while. Are you okay?"

I don't know how to answer. *"Yes, I'm fine?"* He'll know that's a lie. "No, I'm not okay," I finally say, unable to keep the tremble out of my voice.

He opens the door, and I turn my back to him, covering my bare breasts with my arms and looking at him over my shoulder. His blue gaze slides over my body, seeing me naked for the first time in years. "Babe, you can talk to me."

I almost laugh. I can talk to him? Since when? He's finally trying to be the loving mate, the man who understands.

Not hardly.

I tip my head forward, washing the soap out of my hair. It runs down my face, but I don't want to turn and offer him a frontal view of my body.

"It's been a long time, Cain. And we never talked, not ever."

"I know. But I told you things are different now."

"Why? Why now and not back then? And can you close the door? You're letting cold air in here."

"I'm not a drunk now, that's why. I'm not gambling. I spent three years in jail thinking about what I did. That's why." He doesn't close the door.

"But you still have your friend Donovan. He's still calling the shots, right?"

He sighs, leaning in the door. I glance over my shoulder, tossing my wet hair back. "Maybe if we put our heads together, we can figure something out," he tells me.

I hold his eyes for too long. What if he could really be a good man, somewhere down the line? Be a loving husband to someone? Someone who's not me.

But then I remember.

Four people are dead.

Lost cause is written all over this. Some people just don't get happy endings. I decided that a long, long time ago. His best bet is to die of old age in prison, with nothing to comfort him but the memories of what put him there in the first place.

"Maybe so," I sigh.

He finally closes the door, allowing the air to warm up once more. His fuzzy shape opens a linen closet, sets out a couple of towels for me, and then leaves me in the bathroom alone.

He didn't touch me, didn't try to get in with me. I'm relieved and confused at the same time.

After taking as long as humanly possible in the shower, I find him sitting in the living room, alone. I'm wearing pajamas that consist of long pants and a long-sleeve shirt, the most clothes I could justify putting on. Despite the fact that I hate sleeping in pants, I sure as hell won't sleep in panties next to him.

"Brook, I have so much to say, and I don't know where to start." He stares off into space as I sit down beside him.

"Just talk, Cain. We both have things to say, I think."

He glances at me. "You hate me?"

I look up into his eyes, not too quick to answer. "Some, yes. But I think there's a part of me that's deeper and will always remember what you were before all this. I can't forget that. But yes, Cain, hate is there too."

He sighs, resting his head on the back of the couch. "If I could get rid of Donovan, would that help?"

I sit on the couch with a leg tucked under me. "I have no idea."

"The first time I met him, he helped me. He showed me how to stand up for myself when I had no one else. I've never had anyone else, you know? My mom all but left me for all those men after Dad took off. Let those men beat me. I was around twelve then, and that's when Donovan showed up. One used to try to touch me. Fucking pervert. I never would let him though. When that son of a bitch would creep into my room and sit with me, he'd try to put his hands in my pants. I told Donovan about him, and he told me to grab the guy's balls and squeeze them as hard as I could. I was scared shitless, but I did it. He never messed with me again, but he dumped my mom, and she blamed me. After that, I knew it was just Donovan and me. He helped me when the kids picked on me, made me strong. Made me a man. I would've always been scared and weak if not for him, so when you came along, I didn't know any better. I thought he knew best—he always had before."

"But you were always so angry. You were nice to me because you liked me, but I'd see you go apeshit on anyone who crossed you the wrong way." I should've known, should've seen it coming.

"I know. I see things a bit more clearly now, and I'm glad he was there, but I wish he'd moved on. I don't know why he's still here. I don't need him anymore."

I'm reminded of that Disney movie, *Pete's Dragon*. The dragon comes to help the boy because he's orphaned and alone, then moves on at the end of the movie because he's found a happy family finally.

"You think if you finally find your happiness, he'll leave?" It's odd that he thinks their friendship works that way. That Donovan is raising ten kinds of hell to bring Cain his joy and then will just bow out of the picture, like he's some twisted guardian angel and not a sick, fucked-up human being.

He nods. "Yeah. You are my happiness, Brook. I just fucked it all up."

You think? I bite back the sarcasm. He's trying to be open, but unfortunately it's too little, too late. I'm here for one reason, and getting cozy isn't it. "What do you want from me, Cain?"

"Love. Trust. Forgiveness. Anything can be forgiven, can't it?"

I pull back when he reaches for my hand. If I show too much trust too fast, he may not believe it. "I don't know. How do you expect me to believe you're harmless now when you threatened our daughter?"

"It wasn't me, I told you. It was him. I came to help, to keep you both safe." His voice grows thin with desperation.

"But those people died."

"It wasn't me. I've been trying to protect you since I got out of jail. I'm sorry I lost it and hit you that day, but—"

I stand up, walking in circles. "Let me guess—it wasn't your fault. It was my fault for not doing as I was told, or for popping off. It was his fault because he's just an evil bastard, and you can't tell him no.

Never your fault. It's never just because you made a bad choice."

Silence falls between us. He huffs out a breath, watching me walk in circles to nowhere over and over again. I need to keep my mouth shut. It's never done anything but get me into trouble with Cain. I don't know why I never learn.

"You're right. There were times I could've resisted, said no to him. Ignored the taunts and all the bullshit he said to get me riled up, tempting me to get drunk and screw around."

His quiet, defeated tone makes me stop walking. He just admitted fault. Is that what I heard? I turn to face him, finding him on his feet with sad eyes.

"Brook, I'm sorry." His voice cracks.

Damn him, he's going to cry. Looking away, I turn my eyes to the floor. I still hate to see him cry.

"I'm sorry. I'm not good enough for you or her, I know. But I can't let go of you."

He reaches out once more, and this time I don't allow myself to pull away. I let him pull me against his chest into a hug that makes me cry. Not because of where I am, but because of where I'm not. I want these arms to be Brandon's, and this crazy bastard forced me to leave him.

"I know."

"What did you want to say to me?"

I can't remember him ever caring what I had to say about anything. It's almost believable, this whole thing.

"What do you expect from me?"

"What do you mean?"

"Before, I had no say. You already told me that I need to quit my job and don't need a car, so what do I…?" I fade out before I say *"What do I do to avoid your fist?"*

"Just listen to me, and let me take care of you. My buttons are still there, Brook. They haven't changed. Just like I know you're a hothead with a mouth that gets you into trouble. Some things are just what they are."

Are you going to rape me? I wonder if he can see the question in my eyes when I pull back and look up at him.

The conversation dies, and we stare awkwardly at one another, neither of us knowing what to do or say. I believe he's sorry, in his own way. I know he means what he says and has good intentions, but how's that saying go? The road to Hell is paved with good intentions.

"Well, I'm going to go lie down," I finally mutter. Going to bed is the only thing that will keep me out of trouble. My mouth shut, off my phone, the computer. Trying to contact Shane or Ashley or Brandon.

Brandon. Even the thought of him makes me want to ball up right here on the floor and cry. I miss him so much it hurts, only this day-to-day hell looming before me to distract me from what I left behind.

"Okay, I'll lock up. I'm tired too."

My heart stops for a moment. When I go to turn, he grabs my hand, pulling me back toward him. His blue eyes close, and with his hand on my chin, he touches his lips to mine.

Familiar. Memories of first kisses and giggles come with this kiss. Images of sweet sixteen and the prom and the first "I love you." Followed by blood and pain, the barrel of a gun. Hands around my throat.

I don't pull away. I can't. He wants a kiss, so I give him a kiss. It's a peck, lingering for a moment and then pulling away. A soft smile from him is my reward before I turn and head down the hall.

* * *

CAIN

The lack of warmth in her eyes makes me angry. I watch her walk down the hall in those god-awful black plaid pajamas, knowing she's never slept in that kind of shit. She's all wrapped up, hoping I won't touch her.

Ever since I met her, even in the worst times, she slept in panties and a shirt. Sometimes just panties. She hates sleeping in clothes.

I'm so conflicted that I can't think straight and find myself almost wishing Donovan back so I could get clarity from him. I love her, and I need to keep her safe, but I also need her to love me back. Stop all this bullshit.

Right on time, my phone buzzes in my pocket. Even before I pull it out, I know it's him, checking on me.

"What?" I sigh into the receiver.

"How's it going, lover boy?" His laugh makes me grit my teeth.

"You said you'd leave us alone."

"She thinks you're stupid. She thinks she can fool you."

I suck in a breath. "I knew you couldn't stay away too long," I mutter, hoping she won't hear me.

"She's a cocky bitch. Thinks she can fool you into thinking she's happy? That she'll accept you back? Seems like she's forgetting that you know her as well as she knows you."

I fall into the new leather recliner, the craving for a drink swelling in my throat. "I know. You're right."

"It's pissing you off, isn't it?"

Another deep breath. A glance toward the hallway. Anger looms within me like a shadow, creeping into my blood slowly, making everything darker. I clench my fist, crack my knuckles.

"You know what you need to do, don't you? To get all that shit out of her head?"

"Get rid of all those clothes she has, cut her hair. Make her mine again. Wash that old life away," I mutter.

"Have a drink, and then go get that fresh start you wanted so bad. You can't start over if she's lying in bed thinking about him. Get him out of her head."

"You think I'm a fool for this, don't you?"

"Cain, my boy, I'm here to do the thinking for you, remember? Just sit back and do what I say, and everything will be okay. Your wife is trouble, but you can break that. But the girl, she's still small. She still worships you. Don't lose that. How you treat her mother, how you make Mom respect you will mold Carissa. Just because she's here doesn't mean the threat is gone. You can still lose her."

I walk to the kitchen, pull a bottle of whiskey from the cabinet above the fridge, and take a swig from the bottle. It burns on the way down. "I won't lose her, Donovan."

"You're right, because I won't let that happen."

"I don't want you to hurt her."

"Then you better get to work. I'm only here to protect you, remember? I'm the only one who understands. I'm the only one who's ever stayed. I'd never hurt you, Cain."

He'd never hurt me. "I believe you."

By the time I've finished with Donovan, I'm so black inside that I've had too much to drink and hate myself, him, and her too. The only one I don't hate is my child, who's sleeping in the room I put together for her.

I know I have to get Brook back in line, or even

them being here won't protect Carissa. Donovan has made himself clear.

He said she'll listen this time, if I do what he says. The hallway sways beneath me, forcing me to grip the wall as I stumble toward my bedroom. The lights are out, and she has her back to the door, covers to her neck.

I grip the scissors tightly, hoping she won't start screaming and wake up the kid. "Wakey, wakey, little wife," I singsong as I walk around the bed.

Her eyes are shut tight. Pretending to be asleep, surely.

I laugh when they pop wide as I straddle her, rolling her onto her stomach.

"Cain, what are you doing? You said you wouldn't hurt me." Her words are rapid, desperate.

"This won't hurt, baby doll. I promise."

I gather her hair in one hand, long and beautiful. Men love long hair. I bet Brandon did too. Bet he liked to pull her hair when he fucked her.

Can't have that, can we?

I click the scissors together, holding her shoulders down with my knees.

"Please, Cain, don't. My hair… you loved my long hair, didn't you?" she begs.

"I do. I did. But so do all the other men. You're mine now. New life, new look."

"But I grew it out for you, don't you realize that? You love long hair. I was thinking of you," she cries, completely frantic. She tries to turn over, but my weight won't allow it.

Her confession gives me pause, the scissors falling slack in my hand. "You grew it for me?"

"Yes, yes I did. You're my husband, after all." She blinks tears out of her eyes.

He's had his hands in her hair.

The thought forces me to lift the scissors again. He's touched her. I can cut her hair, and she can grow it again; this time it'll be mine alone.

"You shouldn't have let him touch you, Brook."

As the fresh protest stumbles from her lips, I cut her hair off somewhere above the shoulders. A nice, clean cut. Her dark hair springs up, lighter now, fat curls lying on her neck and tears on her cheeks.

I blow out a breath, annoyed with her attachment to something that will grow back. Tossing the handful of hair away, I remember the time I burned her back and raise her shirt. Even in the dark, I can see the scars. She flinches when I run my hands over her back, feeling the scars marring her smooth skin. Her skin is hot and inviting under my hands, making my cock flinch.

God, it's been so long.

"Don't you understand? You will always be beautiful to me, always. You're perfect." I slip my hand up her side, catching the side of a bare breast that's pushed into the mattress.

She doesn't say anything. Her soft sobs say enough.

I shift, allowing enough room to turn her over,

bending closer. "Don't you see how much I love you? Can't you see how much you're hurting me? Everyone hurts me, Brook. Everyone. I just want you to love me."

She nods. I wipe her tears away, wishing she could understand. "Remember what we used to be? Remember high school? How you looked at me made me feel ten feet tall. When we'd fuck in the back of my car, I felt like a man. You did that to me. Remember?"

"I remember. I loved you then."

"You love me now."

No answer.

I pull her shirt up. She just lies there; her arms aren't pinned now. Big breasts, her skin light and bronze as if sun-kissed. It's her natural color, but the thought of her lying in the sun with her tits out both pisses me off and makes me harder than I already am. I run a palm over one, her nipple beading against my skin.

"You've been drinking," she whispers.

"I have."

"Are you going to…?"

I rise to my knees, my hands on my buckle. "Fuck my wife? Yeah, I am."

Her eyes fill with tears and she turns away, pressing them closed. I jump off the bed, yank the covers off her, and pull her pants off. Panties. My pants.

"You're my wife," I remind her again as I climb back into bed.

Chapter Twenty One
BROOKLYN

SON OF A BITCH. IF I HAD THE GUN, or knew where one was, I'd fucking kill him right now. He sleeps the sound sleep of a drunk man who just came. I sit in the shower sobbing, practically scrubbing my skin off my bones, trying to get the phantom remnants of his seed off my body.

I'm in hell once again.

My short hair feels strange in my hands when I touch it, washing it. He told me he'd take me in the morning for a proper haircut—one he approves, I'm sure.

Did Brandon get my note? Did he go to the police? Will they come through this door soon, saving me from this insanity? God, I don't know what to do. But I do know if he wakes and I'm not beside him, I'm in trouble. I turn off the water, dry off and dress how he wants, and climb back into bed in just his shirt and my panties.

Losing my dignity to keep my blood inside my body and my teeth in my mouth.

In bed, the heat comes off him like an oven. With Brandon, I liked that; with Cain, it's just a reminder of where I am, of my captivity. I scoot to the edge of the bed, exhausted but unable to sleep, afraid of what fresh horror I might wake to.

I wonder if Carissa's picking up on any of this. The subtle clues we give off, despite all the efforts to hide reality from her innocence. I can hope that she's just too busy being a kid to notice, putting the questions off for another day. The damage, the repair. How can I even think of helping her recover from this when I can't do it myself? God, if this ever ends, we'll both need therapy.

I toss in the bed, rolling under the covers. Cain is asleep on his back beside me, mouth open, snoring lightly.

I could smother him. Just put the pillow over his face and end it.

No, he's too strong. Too big. I'd never win that fight. Then he'd beat the shit out of me, Carissa would hear us, and she'd ask about my bruises.

No smothering.

How in the hell am I going to get something on him, something worthy of a visit to the police?

I have to get out of here.

* * *

I don't remember falling asleep, but when I open my eyes, the sun's up. Realizing I didn't get up to take Carissa to school, I bolt up in bed and jump to my feet, checking the nightstand for my phone. It's not there.

I check the floor, but it's not there either, nor is it under the bed.

"I got rid of your phone. We'll get you a new one today," Cain says from the door, a cup of coffee in his hand. "Here, baby. How'd you sleep?"

The coffee is for me? That's a first. I take it, simply because I need coffee right now. I could use something way stronger, but that won't help.

"I took her to school, if that's why you're jumping around." He smirks.

"You took her to school?"

"I am her dad, after all. I can manage, you know?"

"Of course." I swallow the coffee, which he's made just how I like it. "What time is it?"

"Ten. I made breakfast too. Come downstairs."

I guess he's trying to make up for last night? No apology, of course. He doesn't think he did anything wrong, but maybe he's feeling guilty for making me feel bad.

He steps up to me, touches my hair. "I'm sorry I had to do this, but…." He pauses, looks into my eyes. "I'll take you out today, get you a new phone, some clothes, your hair done. Just me and you."

He bends to kiss me. For a split second, I almost pull back, slap his face and tell him he had enough of me last night. Then I remember the situation and stop myself. I even kiss him back. The kiss is invasive, gross.

He pulls away, nibbling my lips one last time before smiling. "I'm so glad you're home, babe. Come eat."

"Let me get dressed." I look down at my bare legs.

"Na, I got rid of most of your clothes anyway. You're fine." He takes me by the hand and leads me out of the room.

He got rid of my clothes? Brandon got me so many things I hadn't even worn yet. Now they're all gone.

He's trying to erase the life I built without him.

Downstairs in the breakfast area, he sets a plate of eggs, pancakes, and bacon in front of me before leaning in for a kiss. He stops just short of my lips. "I love you so much." His voice is soft, and it would be nice if I cared two shits.

But I know he loves me. He always has. His own sick version, anyway. Doing the best he can I guess.

Lucky me.

I let him kiss me, but I don't return the sentiment. I'm not really hungry either, more nauseated than anything. Guess that won't be going away anytime soon.

I stuff a bite of food into my mouth, not knowing what else to do. He refills my coffee, then walks out of the room, leaving me to eat.

I can't take this. I just can't. I have to do something.

***

Brandon,

I opened a new email account just to contact you. He knows about my others, and he's been trying to phase out everything I built up while I was away from him. He bought us a big new house, paid cash. The address is 13904 Garden Glen Drive. I'm telling you so you can tell the police. Please don't come here, or you'll risk all our lives.

I'm doing as well as can be expected, I guess. I'd rather not talk too much about it. Just try and get the police here with something so they can take him away. I'm working on it here too, but it's slow going. He's obsessed with making our new life and getting rid of my old one. He hasn't talked about anything else.

Carissa is okay too. She seems to like the new house, easily impressed since she's a young child. Cain gives her anything she wants, of course. I'm grateful she has no real idea what's going on.

He's asleep now, but if I'm gone too long, he'll miss me. I have to get off the computer and delete my history so he won't find this email.

I still love you.

Brook.

* * *

CAIN

My wife forgets that I'm in the computer business; hiding shit from me isn't possible. I stare at the email she sent only hours ago, seething.

Bitch.

She emailed him. Told him she loved him.

I stand up, breaking the laptop screen off the keyboard. I slam the parts against the wall, screaming.

"Cain." I turn at the sound of my name on her lips. She stands in the hallway, wide-eyed. "What's going on?"

"What's going on?" I stomp toward her, grabbing her and slamming her into the wall without thinking. "You emailed him, you bitch! You risk the life of our child? You lied to me?" Spit flies off my lips as I scream at her.

The color draining from her face, she shakes her head but nothing comes out. What can she say?

"You thought I wouldn't find it? You think I'm a fool? A moron?"

"No, I don't think that," she squeaks.

"Well, you must. I'm no fool. Keystroke software, you know. I don't trust you yet. How can I? You've been out acting like a slut, fucking strange men when I was at home waiting for you. And I told you, I *told* you if this shit happened, he would kill her. You risk her life? For a fuck?"

I punch the wall beside her head.

She closes her eyes, bracing for the impact, I assume. "No, I'm sorry. I'm sorry. I don't think you're stupid, Cain. I just need more time, that's all. Just time to settle in. I'm scared."

I lean close to her face. "You should be scared. I'm the only thing standing between you and him, and you keep pissing me off."

She nods, crying again. I'm so tired of it. "Stop crying. You cry all the time. And I saw you crying while we were having sex. You can't hide it from me."

With hasty hands, she wipes her eyes. "Please don't hurt her. Don't hurt me. I'm sorry. Please, we can make this work. Don't hurt her."

"Why? Why must you push me when you know what happens? I don't want to hurt you. Christ, Brook! You're making me do this!" I scream as my head starts to ache, like lightning struck me. I grip her shoulders, the room going dim just as I pull back my fist.

Chapter Twenty Two

CAIN

I GUESS I BLACKED OUT, THOUGH I DON'T know for sure. When I wake up, the color of the light tells me it's midafternoon. I'm in bed, fully clothed on top of the covers. My shoes are still on. A delicate slap to my cheek, my name bubbling out on a panicked voice, forces my eyes open. It's Brook, and she's crying. Her eyes are red and puffy, and her nose is running.

Shit, she has a black eye. Her face is a mess. "What the fuck happened to you?"

"You happened, moron. Get up! She's gone!"

"Me? I didn't hit you. Wait, what? Who's gone?" I bolt up, shaking away the fog in my brain. "Who's gone?"

"Carissa! I went to pick her up from school and she wasn't there. They said she was picked up earlier today. No one could tell me who picked her up. She's gone!"

Gone? Fuck. "Are you sure?"

My answer is another slap and a scream. "Of course I'm fucking sure! I tore that place apart! I almost got the cops called on me for screaming at them. They weren't paying attention. Apparently anyone can just come in and take a kid. Fuck, where is she?" she yells in my face.

My stomach falls into my shoes. "Donovan."

She pales. "He wouldn't really go that far, would he? Not really. He's your friend. She's your child."

I grab her by the shoulders. "I told you he's fucked up, Brook. I have to find him. He's into some dark stuff. Can we talk about this later?"

"Where does he go?"

I have no idea. "I don't know. He comes to me."

She breaks into fresh sobs, slapping at me when I move to hug her. "Leave me alone! This is your fault, damn you!"

My chest tightens. *My little girl. Fuck, what's he doing to her?* "I know."

"Find him."

"I'll try."

"So do it! Find out where she is! Find out what he wants!"

It's her or Carissa. If he gets his hands on Brook, he'll probably kill her.

Do I tell her? If I do, she'll just tell me to take her to him, not realizing what could happen. Or maybe she does realize and just doesn't care. A mother's love.

"You stay here, in case someone calls. I'm going to

go look for her."

"Look where? How can I just sit here and do nothing?"

"You have to. Stay here."

As I walk out, she calls to me. It's the first time she's made me feel needed in years.

I have no idea where I'm going, to be honest. I keep calling to him in my head and out loud, going back to places I've been with him. Nothing. He won't answer me. Not knowing what else to do, I head back home. Pulling onto my street, I see the blue and red lights flashing in my rearview. Glancing at my speedometer, I see I'm not speeding. I wonder why I'm being stopped.

"Cain James?" the officer asks at my window a few minutes later.

Out of the corner of my eye, I see three more cars pull up. Slowly my car is surrounded by cops. *What the fuck?*

"Yeah," I reply warily. "What is this?"

"I need you to come with me. We need to talk to you about your involvement in a few deaths."

Shit. The murders. God, I've been so hung up on Carissa and Brook and making them mine again that I forgot.

I start to move my hands, but he pulls his gun. "Keep your hands on the wheel where I can see them. I'm going to open the door, and you get out with your hands up."

In the end, I'm cuffed and arrested for murder.

They shove me in the back of the police car and drive me to the station. I'm allowed to call my lawyer, who's in Houston and tells me to wait until he gets there. Of course, I'm panicking. My kid is with Donovan, I can't contact Brook to tell her what's going on, and by the time all this is done, everyone may be dead.

Now I'm in a little interrogation room, waiting for someone to come talk to me. Finally, after I've paced a hole in the floor, two detectives come in. One has a laptop with him. The other sets a recorder on the table and introduces everyone for the recording.

I listen to their questions but don't answer. Look at their pictures, no answer. They get annoyed with me, of course. Make their threats, their promises. Then they walk out for an hour or two before coming back. I still don't talk.

I ask them what time it is, if I can make another call, hoping they might allow it. Of course, they say no.

"Mr. James, can you take a look at something for me?" the fat one says. He turns the computer screen toward me. "You see, your mom made a video the day she died. Did you know that?"

"No, I didn't," I say with a tired sigh. Maybe they'll see it wasn't me. Maybe they need me to explain what's on the tape.

"Well, let's watch this, shall we?" He pushes Play.

My mom's face fills the screen, making some adjustments and then backing off before speaking.

"My son is on his way here. Cain James. Coming

to give me a large sum of money that he owes me and has agreed to pay me. I'm recording this because I'm worried. My son has something wrong with him, and he talks to himself all the time. I'm recording this for my own protection, should anything happen. Oh, there's the door. He's here."

A chill runs down my spine at her words. *I talk to myself? That's strange. Why would she say that?*

The positioning of the camera tells me it was sitting on a shelf and I never noticed it.

I watch our interaction, but Donovan isn't on camera. He was there, so where is he? Why can't I see him?

As the moment of her death approaches, I set my face in stone, but my heart is pounding harder and harder as sweat rolls down my sides. *Where in the hell is Donovan? How did he get around the camera? He was standing right behind her.* I remind myself not to show emotion, don't give anything away. But that all melts like butter on a hot knife when I watch myself on camera move forward and break my mom's neck.

I stand, my chair falling to the floor behind me. Watching myself on video, talking to myself, stepping over her body the way Donovan did.

"What did you do to this? This isn't what happened!" I back into the wall, trying to put some distance between myself and this... whatever it is.

It's not me. They did this.

The detective rewinds it, and we watch it again.

Once more, it's not Donovan but me. I go up to my mom, standing behind her, then twist her head just so.

I killed my mom.

My vision goes dim around the edges, my heart beating in my ears so loudly that I can't hear what they're saying to me.

I killed her. Not Donovan.

But I saw him. I saw him do it.

"I saw him. How did you do this? I didn't do this," I mumble.

The detectives look at each other. "You saw who, son?" the older, heavyset one says in a fake fatherly voice.

"Donovan. Donovan killed them all. Not me. I—"

"Here's the thing. We know about Donovan. Your mom also had copies of some of your medical records from when you were a kid. Donovan isn't real. He's in your head. You have schizophrenia, have ever since you were twelve years old."

Schizophrenia. The word buzzes in the air around me.

No.

No.

This isn't real.

Donovan is real.

"She never told me that. She never told me anything was wrong. You're lying. My mom wasn't there, but she would've told me if I had something wrong with me."

Wouldn't she?

He opens a folder that's sitting on the table and hands it to me. Inside are old copies of forms from the doctor she took me to as a kid, after she tried to have me committed. I had no idea what was going on then; the doctor just sat with me and talked to me for a while, and then we left.

His diagnosis is written in barely legible script.

Delusions of a person named Donovan.
Dangerous if not treated.
May require commitment.

I drop the file as if it's burning me, and it slides across the dirty linoleum. "This can't be real. I… I…."
Oh God. Oh fuck.

I start to shake. "I'm not crazy. I'm not crazy. I can see him. I can talk to him." I press my hands over my ears. "I'm not crazy."

"Son, we don't like the word crazy. You have an illness. It's not anything you can help, especially since you had no idea. Your mom didn't do you any favors if she never told you about it. You were a kid, for God's sake. We all believe what we can see, and that's what you did. We understand, really. We aren't here to hurt you. We just want everyone to get the help they need."

I look up into his eyes. Then I remember something, something that makes me want to throw up all over his scuffed-up shoes.

My daughter. Donovan took my daughter. But if he's not real… then who the fuck did it?

Then it hits me, like a blow to the chest.

I blacked out.

I took her.

I start to cry, closing my eyes and covering my ears against Donovan's voice, now laughing at me, taunting me.

He's not real. All this time, he wasn't real. It's been me.

I hurt Brook on my own.

I killed four people.

I kidnapped my own daughter.

I'm a monster. A real monster. There is no Donovan, only me.

My thoughts start to race, adrenaline making my hands shake.

I've been trying to protect Brook from *myself.* I locked her up with the beast and I didn't even know it.

Chapter Twenty Three

CAIN

AS I SIT ON THE FLOOR, SOBBING, THE door opens and my lawyer walks in. "Cain, don't say anything else. These lovely officers have made a mistake. You've been arrested without a warrant. The rookie who brought you in was only supposed to bring you in for questioning, not arrest. I suppose things got mixed up somewhere down the line?" He glares at the officers, who are now looking at each other. He turns back to me and continues. "So your paperwork has been processed, and you're free to go."

I stand up, wiping my eyes. *I can leave? I have to find Carissa. Talk to Donovan.*

Wait… I'm Donovan. Fuck.

God, Brook was right the whole time. I needed help.

Now I need to think. There are only so many places I would go, even as "Donovan."

"Don't go far, son," one of the detectives sneers.

"We're getting warrants right now. It's only a matter of hours."

Hours? By then, this will be over. I know what has to happen now.

My lawyer starts talking to me as soon as we step out of the building, but I don't hear him. His voice hits my ears like buzzing, or that noise the grown-ups make in the Charlie Brown cartoons. I hear what I think is him calling my name as I run off, hailing a cab that's coming down the street. I have to find her.

He is me. I am him.

I sit in the back seat with a blinding headache as I fight to keep him out of my head. *Where would he take her? Where would I take her? Would I really hurt my own kid? Well, fuck, apparently I killed four people, so maybe I would.*

In the midst of my struggle, I work out all the places I go—*we* go. There aren't really that many. The only place I can think of that would be suitable to keep her is the only other place I have access to.

My mom's.

I direct the driver to her address, hoping, fighting my own head, and crying while getting crazy looks from the driver in the mirror.

"Wait for me," I tell him when he pulls in the driveway, leaping from the car and running for the door.

"Carissa?" I shout, my voice shaking. The TV is on; that's a good sign. "Baby, are you here?"

I hear a noise in the kitchen. Inside, I find my five-year-old standing on a chair, struggling to make a peanut butter sandwich at the counter, wide blue eyes turned on me. I can see she isn't sure how to feel. Scared? Relieved?

I run to her, scooping her into my arms. She's rigid, not relaxing as she did the last time. "Baby? Baby, I'm sorry. Are you okay? I didn't mean to…." I don't know how to finish.

"Daddy, can we go home now? I want to go home." She starts to cry in my arms.

"Yes, baby. But I have to take care of something first, okay? Let's go."

I make the driver stop for a Happy Meal, then direct him to Ashley's house. I think that's her name, anyway. We get out of the car, and I crouch on the sidewalk between the driveway and the porch, wiping ketchup off her little face and struggling not to cry. "Baby, do you know I love you?"

She nods.

I don't know what to say, but I have to tell her goodbye. It's the only way. I can't protect them if I'm here, ever. There's no way around it.

"Carissa, I need you to know that no matter what you hear, no matter what happens, I love you so very much. Nothing that happens is your fault. It's all my fault, okay? Can you remember that? You are a good, sweet girl."

"Yes, Daddy."

"Good. Never forget it, okay? No matter what anyone says. You're my baby, and I'm always here with you, okay? I'll always be watching over you, I promise. You can always talk to me."

She nods again, and I pull her into my arms, my last hug. I won't see my baby girl again. It's for the best, but I still struggle to let her go. Knowing I have to, that Donovan can return any minute, I kiss her forehead and lead her to the porch, knocking on the door.

* * *

BROOKLYN

Watching Cain get taken away by the police, just down the street, wasn't the joyous moment I expected it to be, since I don't know where my child is. But they left his car here, and the keys. I spent hours looking for her, everywhere I can imagine she might be, finding nothing. I think about calling the police, but I'm scared. What if calling the police only makes it worse? What if Donovan kills her when he finds out? They would laugh at me for going back to my ex, the one who almost killed me. Probably walk off shaking their heads and thinking we all get what we deserve.

In the end, I don't call them. Maybe later, maybe if

Cain can't find her or Donovan. If he can't get through to Donovan… if… then maybe I'll call.

When darkness falls, I haven't heard from anyone.

I called Brandon, not knowing what else to do. He's sitting with me at home, watching me pace.

"I don't know what to do." I sniffle, crying. "Where could she be? What if she's—"

"She's not. Don't think like that. She's okay," he assures me.

The front door opens, and Cain walks in. My heart stops as I look to Brandon, who shoots out of his chair.

Oh God. What's going to happen?

"Cain…." I look between the men again, reaching into my brain for something, anything.

"Stop. Look, I don't care about this, about him." He waves at Brandon.

Wait, what? He doesn't care?

Frowning, I look at him, my husband. He's been crying, based on his puffy eyes. He's a little pale too.

"Carissa is safe," he starts.

I move to him. "What? Where is she? How do you know? Where?" I grab his upper arms and shake him, as if the answers will tumble out faster.

"She was at my mom's house. I picked her up, fed her, and took her to your friend Ashley's house. She's okay, I promise."

I fall to my knees, sobbing. Neither man moves to comfort me, so I sit on the floor alone, frankly glad no one is touching me. "H-How did you find her?"

Wait, why didn't he bring her home?

Something black falls on me at that thought. A dark expectation. Something horrible is about to happen. He must've wanted her out of the way.

God, is he finally going to kill me?

I scramble to my feet, not knowing what to do, where to cast my gaze.

He sits in the recliner that Brandon was just sitting in, leaning forward, elbows on his knees.

"Brook, the police arrested me for murder, but they had to let me go because they didn't have a warrant signed yet. But they showed me a video and—" His voice breaks, tears filling his eyes. "Long story short, it turns out Donovan isn't real. He's been in my head all my fucking life. My mom got me diagnosed when I was a kid, never told me. All this time…." His voice fades out as he looks up at me, then Brandon, who stands mute by my side.

So he is crazy. But that means….

"Brook, it was me. I guess I must be having a moment of clarity, but I don't know how long it'll last. My mom was scared of me, so she taped our meeting, and it showed me killing her. I swear to God on all I love that I saw him do it. I saw Donovan break her neck. But on that tape, it was me." He sobs, his face now in his hands.

"Cain, maybe we can get you help. They won't convict you for murder. They'll send you to the hospital, right?" I ask.

God, he is crazy.

"Maybe, but I'm not worried about that. I'm a beast, Brook. I meant to love you. I meant to protect you, and all I ended up doing was locking you up with the monster I was trying to protect you from. Fuck, I'm sorry. I didn't know. I swear I didn't know. I tried so hard this time." His shoulders shake as he sobs, broken by the reality that is his twisted mind.

I can't imagine what it must be like to discover that your whole world is a lie. That everything you've known is nothing but psychosis. Finding out the one you've always depended on is all in your head.

I drop to my knees, forcing his eyes to meet mine. His pain hurts me. Despite all my hate for what he's done, knowing what's real and what's not, even if only for a short while, is undoing him—and it hurts me to see it.

"Cain, hey, look at me." His blue eyes shine bright with tears, heavy with sorrow. "You did try. I know you did. Maybe that means you can get better. You didn't know you were sick, all this time. Now you can get some help for it."

He shakes his head. "No, it's too late. I have to protect you and Carissa. I have to. I can't let him hurt you again. Don't you know how much I love you? I've never loved anyone else but you. The moment I saw you, I loved you. When you had my baby, I was so happy. A little piece of our love growing into a person, right?" He smiles for a second. "But I just can't get rid of him, and he'll always hurt you. He's… he's me. I don't even know which one is the real me. He'll come back, and I'll listen to him, because I always have. I always will. But you have to know, please, that I did this for you. To save you… from us."

The finality of his statement makes an alarm go off in my head. I let go of his face as he reaches into the back of his pants and pulls out the gun he took from me.

I scramble back, away from him. *Is he going to kill us all?* I look up at Brandon, holding my breath.

"Hey, man, let's just talk about this," Brandon says, taking a step toward me.

Cain moves the weapon from hand to hand, back and forth. "Brook, what will you tell Carissa about me when she's bigger?"

Carissa? Oh God… he's not going to kill us.
He's going to kill himself.

I don't know what to do. It's not going to happen. It can't. It has to be some kind of manipulation.

But what if it's not?

I can't get a good breath, and panic is seizing my heart, causing it to beat in a heavy, irregular rhythm. "Cain, you can tell her yourself. She can see you when you're better, talk to you on the phone."

"No, I can't. She's better off this way. Safer. Brandon…."

Brandon frowns at him, staring at the weapon as he pulls me behind him.

"Brandon, do you love her? My wife?"

I start to cry. *This can't be happening.*

"Yes, I do love her. Don't do this, man. We can get you help. You'll feel better. You're just not thinking straight right now."

Cain stands up. "No, I won't. I won't feel better. And do you know why?" He paces, shouting now. "Because I'm fucking crazy. I've done nothing but hurt everyone who's ever loved me. I'm a monster. There's no saving me. How can you save me when the monster lives in my head? You can't protect me from it. No one can. I'm thinking clearly for the first time."

Cain grabs Brandon by the arm. "You'll take care of them, right?"

"Don't do this."

"It's the only way I can protect them. It's the only way I can show them I love them. Tell me you'll take care of them, both of them. Tell my daughter I loved her. That I'm sorry, that I did everything I knew how to keep her safe. Promise me you'll tell her." Tears stream down Cain's face. "Oh, I almost forgot." He half laughs, staring into my face as if it's the last time. "When I got out of jail, I was the one who told them to call you. I made the arrangement. I wanted you to be safe from Donovan... before I knew the truth."

I shake my head, mute verbally but screaming internally, unable to process this moment.

"You'll tell her?" He turns back to Brandon.

"I'll tell her," Brandon whispers.

I step out, shaking Brandon off when he tries to pull me back. I look up into Cain's face—the man I loved, chose, my first everything. "Please, don't leave me like this," I say, unable to keep the desperation out of my voice. "You can't do this to me. I loved you. I left my family for you. We fucked everything up. I didn't send you to get help, and you didn't know you needed it. Don't fucking leave me like this! Don't leave *her*! What do I tell her? How can I tell her that her daddy is dead when she just found him again? How can you do that to her? To me?" I scream at him. I hit his chest with my fist, then shake him, but he just cries.

"I'm sorry. Tell her I didn't know any other way. I'm sorry."

"Don't leave me!" I reach for the gun, but Brandon pulls me back, and Cain pushes me into his arms. "No! You can't do this, Cain! I still love you! I forgive you. Don't go!"

"I know." He sobs, smiling. His kiss is salty when he plants it on my lips. "Thank you, baby. I love you."

Brandon locks me in his arms, and Cain walks out the front door. I almost miss the sound of the gunshot because I'm too busy screaming.

Then everything goes silent.

***

He really did kill himself in the front yard. I keep

telling myself that. It's been weeks now, and it still doesn't seem real. He's gone, finally gone. It's not the ending I wanted, but it's the one I got. Turns out he loved me after all.

Now that it's over, and I can stop on my way to work and see his grave, I can tell him that I wished Donovan had been real. Maybe then there might've been a shot at coming out of this a different way. But we're safe now. I don't have to look over my shoulder anymore. I can look at Brandon and tell him I love him now. I'm getting help with my issues, and so is Carissa, and Brandon's there to help us both through it as we go.

I've found the life I wanted all along, and I'm not hiding from anyone. I'll never hide from anyone ever again. This has changed me forever. I'll never be the same person I was before Cain James walked into my life, giving me that look and that smile. But that's what love does, doesn't it? It changes everything.

In the afternoon sun, Brandon holds me against his chest as I stare at the stone with Cain's name on it, wondering if my feelings toward his death will always be so confused. I don't leave flowers or anything like that. Instead, I just tell him I love him, and that Carissa loves him still. When it came down to it, I really did love him. He just hurt me more than he ever loved me back.

They say love isn't supposed to hurt, that hate has no place in love.

What the hell do they know?

The End

NOTE FROM THE AUTHOR

As a former 911 emergency operator, I know firsthand that stories like this one happen every day—domestic violence, mental illness, suicide. People who don't know they need help, don't know how to get it, or are too far gone to know what to do. If you or someone you know needs help, there is help out there. You can contact your local police department for resources, or click on the following links:

HELP FOR MENTAL ILLNESS:
WWW.NAMI.ORG

HELP FOR DOMESTIC VIOLENCE:
WWW.THEHOTLINE.ORG/

HELP FOR THE PREVENTION OF SUICIDE:
WWW.SUICIDEPREVENTIONLIFELINE.ORG

Do not be ashamed to ask for help, to reach out. Someone out there understands, and you are never alone.

#endthestigma

THANKS

Thanks for reading *BREAK MY BONES*. I do hope you enjoyed my story. I appreciate your help in spreading the word, including telling a friend. Before you go, it would mean so much to me if you would take a few minutes to write a review and share how you feel about my story so others may find my work. Reviews really do help readers find books. Please leave a review on your favorite book site.

Don't miss out on New Releases, Exclusive Giveaways, and much more!

JOIN MY NEWSLETTER: WWW.RACHAELTAMAYOWRITES.COM/
CONTACTME
LIKE ME ON FACEBOOK:
WWW.FACEBOOK.COM/RACHAELTAMAYOWRITES

JOIN MY READER GROUP:
WWW.FACEBOOK.COM/THERTASYLUM/

FOLLOW ME ON TWITTER:
@RTAMAYO2004

FOLLOW ME ON PINTEREST:
WWW.PINTEREST.COM/RACHAELTWRITES

Rachael Tamayo was born and raised in Texas and has a unique insight into mental illness due to her former twelve years in law enforcement. She enjoys weaving both the darkness and the hope of humanity into her books.

ACKNOWLEDGMENTS

I would first like to thank my family and friends. Those who watch my moods change with the pace of the writing of the book, and especially those who I call my sounding boards and brainstorming partners. You keep me sane! Thank you to my PA, who keeps me on track and takes care of all the little things for me—I can't keep up without you! Huge thanks to the Tangled editors who combed over this book and helped me make it shine. My biggest thank you is to the readers. Without you, these stories would still be swirling inside my brain. I am so grateful to you! For more information on me, my books, or just to reach out and say hello, please head over to my website, www. RachaelTamayowrites.com

DISCOVER

LAST NIGHT - Kim Deister

What do you do when you keep losing time?

Terrifying visions torment Starra. Lost moments of time and flashes of images too horrific to accept fill her with icy fear so complete she can't escape it. With too many unanswered questions, she needs answers. Now. It's her only hope if she wants to save what's left of her shattered mind and soul.

Unlike Starra, Mina cares nothing for her soul. Damned long ago, she's too scarred for redemption. There are people meant to enjoy lives of love and family and friends. Mina isn't one of these people. Her life is in the shadows, unafraid of the dark... until she realizes that something lurks in those shadows, something that wants to tear her apart.

One never knows what the darkness hides...

A Divided Mind - M. Billiter

Sometimes that little voice in your head isn't always yours.

What if the only friend you have isn't real? When the voices in his head begin to make sense, high school senior Branson Kovac turns to the one friend he's still got… only to discover he's not really there.

NOTHING HIDDEN EVER STAYS - HR Mason

A two-hundred-year-old curse. A tangled thread of mental illness. A growing list of Ross family women dying young. The house where it all began, Desolate Ridge, holds all the secrets.

Abandoned at a hospital when she was only three years old, Aubrey Ross grew up as a ward of the state, passed from one foster family to the next. Having endured years of abuse and neglect, she's become hardened to the world around her.

She's flirted with depression and anxiety, and she's haunted by premonitions. When a strange man approaches Aubrey with information about her past, she knows her life is about to change. Inside the envelope is the deed to a house in Ohio—her ancestral home.

When Aubrey arrives in Rossdale, the town named

after her family, she immediately experiences situations she cannot explain. She hears voices, sees apparitions, and has vivid visions of tragedies she can scarcely comprehend. Aubrey comes to realize she is reliving events which have happened to those who came before her.

Then she meets Hank Metzger, the town's sheriff, whose family has an eerie connection to her own. As the secrets of Desolate Ridge are unearthed, Aubrey begins to understand her destiny is tied to Hank's in a way she cannot escape.

ABOUT THE PUBLISHER

As Hot Tree Publishing's first imprint branch, Tangled Tree Publishing aims to bring darker, twisted, more tangled reads to its readers. Established in 2015, they have seen rousing success as a rising publishing house in the industry motivated by their enthusiasm and keen eye for talent. Driving them is their passion for the written word of all genres, but with Tangled Tree Publishing, they're embarking on a whole new adventure with words of mystery, suspense, crime, and thrillers.

Join the growing Hot Tree Group family of authors, promoters, editors, and readers. Become a part of not just a company but an actual family by submitting your manuscript to Tangled Tree Publishing. Know that they will put your interests and book first, and that your voice and brand will always be at the forefront of everything they do.

For more details, head to
WWW.TANGLEDTREEPUBLISHING.COM.

CPSIA information can be obtained
at www.ICGtesting.com
Printed in the USA
LVHW111724091019
633689LV00003B/600/P

9 781925 853520